Howlet was remembering the girl who'd turned to peer at him from the porch of Tigley's store, feeling again those unwanted emotions, recalling what he had seen of her face. She had been too intent, too completely absorbed, for her interest to have stemmed from idle curiosity. In back of the wonder and worry he was sure of, there'd been something, he thought, which had been very like fright.

He put her out of his mind. A man with his record had no right to think of women. Not decent ones.

Nelson Nye

CHARTER
NEW YORK

A DIVISION OF CHARTER COMMUNICATIONS INC.
A GROSSET & DUNLAP COMPANY

LONG RUN
Copyright © 1959 by Nelson Nye

An ACE CHARTER Book

Published simultaneously in Canada
Manufactured in the United States of America
68097

ONE

THE dusty sag-shouldered shape in the Mexican saddle of a deep-breathing dun came out of the brush with a grunt of relief, pulling up just short of the slope's naked rimline. There, fumbling Durham and papers, he put together a smoke in the sun's last light while his glance took stock of the hogbacks and gulches, mesas and canyons, which cut up that vast spread of country behind him—a habit he had been at some pains to avoid.

He was a leather-cheeked man in worn workaday clothing, thorn-clawed and faded. Weariness had settled bone deep in the folds of him, and something else, not so easily defined, a kind of sourness of phlegm developed from thoughts too often gone over to be constructive or healthy. Hate was a part, yet was not the true base, of it. Disgust was there too, and rebellion. All his troubles—and he was aware of this—could be tracked straight back to his dexterity at triggering sudden death from a six-shooter. It was a talent he possessed and had deliberately perfected through the smoke and yelling terror of the lately finished Rustlers' War. The mark of

1

those years was in his tight lips, and in his bleak, windswept, unfathomable stare.

"Will" his mother had named him. "King of the Corpsemakers" they called him in Texas; and there were those who'd used other and less flattering names. He'd been regarded as a fool for riding out of the fight empty-handed. Mostly, though, the ones who had known him had called White Howlett *gawd-awful sudden with his equalizer,* these having in mind the loss of some loved goner.

Few now remembered the boy he had been, hard working, hard riding, a real card at a frolic such as neighbors used to have to get up a barn or break in a new house. Those who had known him remembered only that gun. It was a country where old wounds scabbed and broke open, exposing the ugliness festering within.

He'd had too much pride to let hard feelings move him, but he had moved all the same. The hate went too deep, and too many damned fools coveted the reputation envisioned as belonging to the gun that cut him down. It was kill or be killed, and so he'd got out.

He crossed East Texas to the Red River country. He went north, went south—clean south to Corpus, to Fort Stockton, Brady and San Saba —clean into the windblown starkness of Caprock.

He saw a mort of country, did a heap of riding. But the most that he got out of it was a revoltingly bitter truth: A man carried his own hell with him.

He could not disguise or dissemble, or even hide for long, the things which pushed and pulled at him. Gunsmoke smell was an acrid stench that eventually bred its own fresh violence. Howlett had learned to live with this as one learns to live with an incurable disease, giving it his food, half his bed, wrapping himself in the hard shell of self-sufficiency, afraid to put down roots, afraid of friends, trusting no one— himself least of all.

He'd put Texas behind, not with fresh hope but with a kind of desperation. He never stayed anyplace for long. He lived in an almost continual state of motion, eternally drifting, more a shadow than a man. Many times he'd swapped horses, casting off at each stop with a change of name some portion of the last identity. The pattern of his travels was deliberately erratic. He'd gone unshaved; he'd shaved meticulously. He'd grown a beard, many styles of mustache.

He'd tried trapping, a little mining; swung a bull-whip with a freight hitch. The one thing he'd kept strictly away from was cattle.

That was in New Mexico.

For three weeks now he'd drifted west across Arizona, replacing one by one the various items of his apparel. He was a cowhand, not trying to catch on, content to ride chuck line and be thought a goddam saddle tramp. He *hoped* this was how folks regarded him. Several times here of late he'd been treated with fishy stares, and one practical-minded crusty old man had out-and-out asked what price he'd put on his gun in the event of possible trouble over water in the neighborhood. Howlett had quit that place as though he'd picked up a rattler.

Thus his days were spent, a masterless man carried wherever the winds chanced to waft him —"too proud to cut hay and not wild enough to eat it."

Paused now, peering off across the mingled reds and yellows and the deepening blues and purples of all that layered earth and rock, he could find no indication that anyone was watching him; yet this brought no lift of spirit, no comfort or reassurance. He was done with hope; there was no trust in him; all the faith he had was blindly warped into what experience had shown he could do with his pistol.

He sighed in sudden realization. Looking back was no good. Looking back was a recognized hallmark of a fellow on the run. He could understand this, yet completely fail to grasp that where the mind went there the man was also.

He stubbed out his smoke against the horn of the saddle, got down and picked up the hoofs of his horse. This dun was of that color called *bayo coyote,* dark maned, buckskin with zebra marks about the knees and hocks, a dark stripe outlining the bony ridge of its spine; an animal descended from a breed of Spanish ponies particularly noted for early speed and great endurance. Good traveler, easy keeper, deep through the girth and broad of chest, with hoofs grown hard as flint in this dryness.

He considered the silence, got into the saddle. Blind Mule, he recalled from the talk of an Ox-tail puncher, shouldn't be far from his present whereabouts, a mining town serving as source of supplies for the ranches of this region. He recalled the brands of cattle he had noticed: X Bar, Star Cross, Tadpole, 310 and Two Pole Pumpkin. Fed up with his own company, he welcomed the thought of a night in town, though his mind continued to turn it over for possible aspects of danger.

There were no rewards hung up for him. He found a certain dry irony in the sour reflection that he was probably about as *un*wanted a jasper as a man could find in a couple of days' riding. There was of course his reputation, which may or may not have got this far. It did not seem too brash to ride in so long as he kept his hat on.

Still, he sat a while longer, moodily eyeing the possibilities, finally with a shrug removing pistol and shell belt, thrusting them into the tied folds of the slicker he had wrapped about his blankets. He wasn't at all sure where to look for this town but thought if he got high enough he might be able to spot it. He set the buckskin at the slope's rising tangents, sighting on where the green fluted shape of a three-armed saguaro stood lonely sentinel against the sky.

The sun was lowering rapidly now, shafting the clouds with its flood of red gold, turning them into great slabs of bright copper. A breeze was curling up out of the canyons and somewhere a hawk cried as Howlett, rimming out, caught a breath-taking glance at the country beyond.

Much of it, vaguely blue, lay half lost in shadow—dark tumbled masses of ravine and butte, distantly freckled by jade dapples of pine, spruce and other growth. Howlett sat there, drinking it in, awed by such magnificent desolation, by the wild splendor of it, hidden and protected by the towering shapes of the roundabout mountains. A waiting land, remote and lonely.

He picked out then the roofs of the town, gray scattered dabs more glimpsed than seen through a tangle of branches several hundred feet below, perhaps two miles away by trail. The raw lighter gashes in that crazy quilt of purpling shadows would be mine dumps. Where there were mines there would be men and plunder. Unwillingly he carried the thought a little further, knowing that where there was plunder there would be those who congregate in its vicinity, and, inescapably, violence.

A windless chuckle faintly reshaped his lips, and this thin smiling clung to their outer contours as he straightened to go on. He was lifting the reins, still looking around, the wild face of the region queerly gripping and exciting him, when a gun split the quiet. Almost at once the sound was duplicated. Tangled echoes, thinly stretched and breaking, came up out of the shadows like the snapping of dry sticks. If there were hoofbeats he didn't hear them.

On guard, he heard the yammer of those shots

climb through a dozen canyons. His shoulder muscles drew more narrowly together as his glance went at the curdles of gloom flatly filling the broken run of this picture. The shots had come from somewhere below; that was all he knew. And then he shook his head, realizing he had not been their target.

Common sense, that cold clutch of reason, got him half turned around, but Howlett swung back with bared teeth, ignoring the caution that would have rooted him there. Even as blind fear cried its despair of him, he was putting the buckskin down into the shadows, threading the foliage that slapped and whipped at him. He wasn't being quixotic—neither mercy nor charity had anything to do with it. He had to go down there. He had to know more because, whatever he did, he was caught in this now. He had been too near. It was too late to find and rub out his tracks—he may even have been seen. To cut and run could get him blamed, get him saddled with violence. Better to take this calculated risk, to face up to the facts of what had happened than be trailed by them, perhaps pushed into a noose.

It never occurred to him that shots might have some innocent explanation, might in fact have been fired at game. Howlett's acquaintance with trouble had been too thorough, too all-inclusive, to doubt that a man had been killed down there.

It was impossible for him with any haste to reach the place without sending ahead of him the rumor of his approach. There were too many rocky outcrops, too much brush to be got through. He made noise. He had been too long familiar with this kind of thing to allow the racket to get out of hand; but there was enough, he reckoned, to give the one who had done the shooting plenty of chance to get under cover.

And so it was with considerable astonishment that he came suddenly on the place he was hunting only to find it—a small clearing brownly carpeted in needles—still inhabited. A fellow with his back toward Howlett was tying a corpse belly-down across a snorting, bridling, very much distressed pony. A second dead shape had already been lashed to another fidgeting mount securely tied nearby. A third horse, a blue roan apparently belonging to the one who was readying the stiffs for travel, stood nervously blowing, hitched to the ground by trailing reins.

None of this—including Howlett's arrival, which he must certainly have noted—appeared at all to perturb the man. He said, without bothering to look around, "Hang onto that roan if you want to make yourself useful."

The roan was no scrub. Clean-limbed legs, deep through the heart and powerfully quartered with a long underline that promised speed in addition to bottom. A Steeldust, Howlett figured. Very nearly the equal of his own horse.

Howlett's rifle lay across his thighs. Most of his attention was put to watching the man. The fellow worked with a deft sureness; he was an expert with knots. He had on good boots, probably hand-stitched Hyers—expensive. He wore serviceable range clothes that, although the common run with cow folks, were more remindful of town duds on a prosperous rancher. He appeared to be solidly put together, muscular without growing to beef, thick necked with a skull that went up like a cliff from the back of his collar, with a scraggle of cornsilk hair thinly showing.

Howlett, hunched like a spring, was poised for whatever might come of this meeting, a little baffled to find murder so indifferent to discovery.

Finished, the man turned, coolly looking Howlett over. "You live around here, I guess— know the country. . . ."

He continued, when Howlett didn't answer, to inspect him. Deep-chested, compact, wholly assured, the fellow might be anywhere from twenty-six to forty. He seemed endowed with a restless energy that came out of him even when he stood completely still. He was plainly accustomed to making big tracks, and showed a Caesar's features, attractive when he smiled as he did now, still eyeing Howlett.

"No point in getting your back up. That pair got off cheap, considering the trouble they've put me to." He brushed back his coat to show the flash of a badge. "Been camping in their tracks for over a week now—thought I had them twice. They been passing the queer—like to ruined the Douglas bank."

"Counterfeiters?"

"You can't go by looks. Those two were about as slick as they come in that line. Regular double-actin' engines." He walked over to the roan. "Look at this," he said, opening a pair of bulging saddlebags. He held up several packets of crisp banded banknotes. "Tens." The bags were crammed with them. "Can't tell 'em from the real thing without you've got a glass and know exactly what to look for." He scowled, staring off through the trees. "Damned etcher got away from me—"

"Etcher?"

"Feller that made the plates. Cretch there and Crispen furnished the press, the paper and inks. Touch-and-go thing. I've only got one pair of eyes in my head."

"I thought U.S. marshals generally fetched them back alive."

"Marshals is people too." The man spat. "I damn near crawled right into their gun barrels— I'd left the roan back a piece, trying to spot 'em. If you want to check up go ahead, you'll find the place. Down there in that mountain mahogany." He dredged up a hard grin. "When it boils down to me or a pair on the wing, I generally figure to make sure it ain't me. Etcher was mounted; time I got round to him he was going like he was trying to keep step with a twister."

He tipped back his head and took a scrinch at the sky. "Now I've got to get after him. How far to the nearest town?" he asked suddenly.

"Down in the basin four-five miles."

"Want to take this pair of stiffs in for me? Or would that be going too much out of your way?" Howlett didn't show much enthusiasm. The badge packer said, "I can't leave 'em here." He got into his saddle, peering off through the trees again. "If I don't come up with that bugger before it gets dark . . . What's the name of that town?"

"Blind Mule."

"Just leave 'em with whatever law they've got. You can tell him I'll . . ." He got a dog-eared notebook out of his coat and, wetting a thumb on his tongue, flipped the pages. "Here—Blind Mule. Jim Vaguely, sheriff's deputy. Tell him I'll stop by for them tomorrow. Better put 'em in the icehouse—and tell him I said to get hold of the coroner."

Howlett was only about half listening. A considerable proportion of his wandering attention was taken up with the picture of himself coming into a strange town to hunt up the law with a couple of stiffs packed face down across saddles. It brought a thin rash of sweat against the clutch of his collar. But how could he refuse without inviting the man's suspicion?

While he was lost in the complexities of this, and before he could find any firm ground to stand on, the tinbadge, taking Howlett's compliance for granted, began cruising along the scuffed ground into timber. He lifted a hand. "See you tomorrow."

So Howlett was stuck with it.

Casting back, trying to discover where he could have done any differently, he had a sharp, gnawing conviction of trouble. It wasn't anything he could take up and feel. More a smell,

11

far off and faint, as of skunk. Unmistakable.

He kept pushing it around. Even if that deputy got up on his high horse, he would have to climb down when the marshal came in. But Howlett continued to be increasingly disturbed. The thing that really graveled him was the notice of what that tinbadge was letting him in for—a man might as well come blowing a trumpet as put into a strange town towing two dead men.

He was sorely tempted to turn loose of the chore. As a stranger Howlett was vulnerable— doubly so if they got onto his identity. The last thing he'd wanted was to be put in the position of having to give an account of himself.

The town, when he reached it, well past full dark, looked not greatly different from the one fleeting glimpse he'd had of Bisbee in passing. Though it was used as a base of supply by ranchers, it was plain that copper was king around here. The main street—and the only one that could truly be called a street—was three blocks long, bent five times by the convolutions of the gulch and petering out at both ends into a kind of ramshackle collection of jerry-built squatter shacks, grayed by weather and huddling like sheep. Lights winking down from the surrounding slopes told of other buildings of less determinate character. The three blocks taken over by the marts of trade and pleasure were bright with lamp and lantern light when Howlett appeared with his dead freight.

He did not at first attract much notice. The potholed way was thick with churned dust so that traffic—and there was a deal of it—was forced to move through a kind of lemon fog greatly favoring concealment of identity. People caught out in this were mostly too miserable to be greatly interested in those they brushed elbows with. A further distraction was the peril of numerous heavily loaded ore wagons which gave right of way to no one. By the time he had got as far as the post office, which was in the town's largest general store Tigley's Mercentile —midway of the second block, Howlett had passed seven saloons, a bake shop, three honky-tonks and two poolrooms.

The board walks were jammed with a noisy miscellany of pedestrians—bearded and earth-stained hard-rock men. Orientals with the bottoms of their loose shirts flapping, Cornish timbermen, mule skinners, cowhands, a pair of trappers with ringed tails dangling from their coonskin caps, three blueclad troopers from some nearby post, and even a sprinkling of hard-faced women. Eight stolidly staring blanket-wrapped Apaches squatted against the near wall of the Mercantile, the black braids of their hair weirdly powdered with dust.

A group of big-hatted cowmen had their heads together where the shadows were deepest at the far end of Tigley's porch. Howlett's glance, swinging back from them, crossed and was stopped by the look of a woman who, having just climbed the steps, now wheeled in the light of the door to peer around at him. Her hair, pulled severly back in a bun, was as startlingly red as a cardinal's breast. By no wildest stretch of imagination could she ever have been called pretty or even handsome. The ridges of bone in her face were too prominent, her mouth was too wide, her jaw too determined. But she was young and she was astonished, her interest very genuine; and her shape called up in Howlett feelings he had thought long since to have scoured out of him.

As swiftly as she had turned, the woman swung away and went into the store. Howlett held his place a moment longer; then the crush of traffic moved him on. Beyond the Mercantile —with CLARA—EATS at his left and GUN SHOP, E.S. BOLTON, PROP. narrowly facing it between the BUCKEYE SALOON and MINER'S REST—traffic snarled again. A dozen languages helped to garble the talk flowing round him like the racket of locusts. There a barker hawked the delights of Fat Emmas's and three black-coated gamblers shoved past on the walk. Blind Mule was booming. No doubt about it.

A wagonload of undressed planks, some of them already beginning to warp, was stopped directly in front of Howlett. A rattling string of empty high-sided freight wagons with six-foot wheels went rumbling by on his left, ballooning up fresh whorls of the stifling ocher-colored dust, every wheel rim dripping trails of pulverized earth. A ragged barefooted fellow, a bloody blade in his fist, suddenly came up under the dun, dived forward and scrambling between two sets of those wheels, reappeared momentarily in front of Clara's and incontinently vanished.

"Who you got there, pardner?" someone called from the right. Howlett, twisting his head, got a look at bright eyes in a curious face that, round as an apple, supported a brown derby and the promising first crinklings of a handlebar mustache.

"Couple of gents who didn't make it. Where'll I find the sheriff's deputy?"

"That'll be Jim Vaguely—last block, west side of the street," the derby called after him as northbound traffic commenced once more to crawl.

With the lumber wagon still jouncing in front and the plodding work stock of a dray piled high with barreled beer almost tromping the heels of the buckskin, Howlett snail-aced along until, some ten minutes later, he saw the word JAIL daubed in fat letters across the front of a snake-thin tin-roofed building sandwiched between the BUCKET OF SUDS and the eight-foot front of TOM KELLY'S PLACE. Pulling his led horses after him, he drove into the southbound congestion and bulled his way through, ignoring the shouts and angry curses of those who were compelled to pull up to let him by.

The jail must have been an afterthought, wedged in by necessity long after the rest of the buildings were up. About forty feet deep, it was scarcely ten wide, constructed of what looked to be mine timbers set up cheek by jowl and banded together with scraps of old iron. Two slotlike windows without gratings or glass were high up on either side of the plank door which, open, let out a spill of guttering light from a smoke-blackened lamp bracketed above a battered rolltop desk.

Howlett swung down, seeing nobody in there. He hauled his horses into an alley, tying their reins to iron rings in the jail wall. Walking back to the front he stepped inside, glad to get off the street, gladder still to get away from his freight.

Another door, closed, barricaded the back. "Anybody home?" Getting no answer, he tried this door but found it barred. It didn't even have a latchstring. He called again, louder, disgustedly shaking it. When still nothing happened he shook it again. A peephole slot had been cut head-high in the width of this barrier, a piece of cast iron swiveled onto the back. This was now swept aside to disclose the top half of a man's whiskered face. "How many times you fellers got to be told? No visitin' after sundown! You wanta gab with Dollarosa—"

"Sheriff's deputy I'm looking for."

"You won't find him here." Whiskers sniffed, and put an end to the discussion by closing the slot.

The grim cast of Howlett's features became a little more pronounced. He was heartily tempted to shake the dust of this place, but cooler thinking prevailed. He had already trekked more than twelve hundred miles, and nothing which mattered had been noticeably improved except the possibility of disassociating himself with past violence. Here he was simply a new face among scenes where new faces were an accepted part of the view.

In the noisy confusion of this remote copper camp it was the *now* which most counted, few having the time, inclination or energy to be very strenuously concerned with what a man had put behind. Howlett realized that most fellows, saddled with this freight and given the reception he'd got from Whiskers, would have washed their hands of the business. He was not quite sure he could afford such independence. The marshal had clearly seen him—that derby-hatted gent too. No telling how many others had noticed the company he kept. He found it hard to decide what course around here would seem normal. It was the familiar, the repeated sequence, which generally provoked the least regard. In a camp of this kind a couple of stiffs shouldn't be too uncommon a sight. Likely nobody but the marshal would give a damn what became of them—or him either.

But this was the rub. Every turn Howlett took brought him back to that badge toter. The man was nobody's fool. He was cold as a well chain.

Howlett stepped outside, eyes thinly narrowing. He was cut off from his horse by a muttering crowd that, still growing, blocked the mouth of the alley.

"All right—break it up!" a man shouldering into them nervously commanded. "What's goin' on?" Talk fell away. The speaker disappeared among the jostling shapes and shadows. His voice incredibly lifted. "God of Golgotha! Who — How'd— Where'd *they* come from?"

Over their heads, from the stoop, Howlett said, "Is that Jim Vaguely?"

"Eh? . . . That's right," the newcomer said, twisting around. Coming through the crowd he was presently in sight again, peering up at Howlett after the manner of one who has been thoroughly shaken.

The whole feel of this deal, Howlett realized, was wrong: the crowd, the gray-cheeked deputy, the constrained and utter stillness with which everyone regarded him. *How* wrong he didn't know until he'd said, "I fetched them in," and found himself confronted with the muzzle of Vaguely's pistol.

He pulled a thin breath through the constriction of his throat. "What's that for?"

"Get them paws up!" Vaguely said.

"I'm not heeled—"

"Mister, don't argue! Just get 'em up and get back into that office."

There was in Howlett a wicked impatience with the whole extent of this foolishness, but he could see that the deputy was thoroughly serious. Because he had no choice, Howlett did as he was bidden, even grinning a little as he raised his hands in a kind of embarrassed, self-conscious fashion. The doorway filled with glowering faces.

"Where is it—what'd you do with it?"

A cold pit formed in Howlett's belly. He didn't like the careless way the upset deputy was brandishing his pistol. "If I knew—"

"Don't twist words with me!"

Howlett didn't miss the almost furtive way the deputy's eyes kept slanching around at those faces in the doorway. He said, "Those two stiffs aren't worth half the sweat you seem to be giving this."

A growl swelled out of that group around the door.

Vaguely said. "You want a rope around your neck?"

"Not particularly." Howlett sighed. "I was up on the west rim," he said, and wondered how far he should go trying to clear himself. He still couldn't believe he stood in any real danger. This whole thing was too much like a woman's hysterics. Tomorrow the tinbadge would take him off the hook; but another look around the room gave him no reason to imagine he had that much time. Without mentioning his background, he gave the whole story of how he had come to fetch in those shot hombres. Even to his own ears it didn't sound too likely. He saw the skeptical looks, the belligerent scowls. "According to that marshal," he said doggedly, "there was three of them."

"But all you saw was the pair you brung in."

"That's right. I saw tracks going into the timber, though."

Vaguely, scowling, chewed at his cheek.

"After you heard them shots you claim you never heard no sound of a getaway." This from one of the fellows in the bunch around the door.

Another gent said, "Sounds fishy as hell!" And the look of the rest of them endorsed his opinion.

The deputy considered Howlett dubiously. "An' he asked you to fetch these two dead fellers in so he could be free to push after this other guy." He stared a long time. Over his shoulders the others watched Howlett with a growing impatience.

A gangling man growled, "What was the name of this marshal?"

Howlett shook his head. "He said to put these stiffs on ice . . . that he'd be coming in tomorrow. And he asked me to tell Vaguely to get hold of the coroner."

Vaguely threw up his hands, then jerked his gun back in line.

"Let's string him up an' get it done with," somebody shouted.

The gangling man growled, "We've heard enough of his lies."

Vaguely flourished the gun. "He's goin' into the pen till I get at the straight of this."

A man who looked like a blacksmith asked, "You don't believe that crap, do you?"

"I believe this feller run into *some*body. Why else would he bring Cretch and Crispen in? If he had killed them hisself—"

"He had plenty of reason—"

"If *you* had dropped them," Vaguely said, "would *you* come packin' them in?"

An uncomfortable look touched a few of the

faces. The soot-smeared one Howlett took for a blacksmith grumbled: "All I know is, they're dead and this guy shows up with them. We got enough fellers to hold a miners' court right now—"

"String him up!" one of them yelled, and a dozen others echoed it.

The gangling miner who had asked for the marshal's name cried bitterly, "If these damn drygulchin's ain't stopped pretty quick . . ."

He let the rest of it go as the back door swung open to show the whiskered jailer grinning above the barrels of a sawed-off Greener. "Use a little help, Jim?"

"Get those fellers out of here."

There were growls and muttered curses, but no one seemed inclined to make a test case of what could be done with that shotgun. Vaguely shut the street door, driving home the iron bar doing service as a bolt, stood watchfully wiping the sweat off his neck while the jailer slapped Howlett over for weapons, then waved him on through into the barred cage Whiskers unlocked and slammed back of him.

Vaguely put away his six-shooter. "What did that feller look like?"

Hard, competent, Howlett remembered. "Like a marshal," he said.

"Describe him."

"Plenty of weight through the shoulders, thick neck but no fat. About my height, little heavier maybe. Had a nose like a hawk."

Vaguely and the jailer swapped widening glances.

"Notice his eyes?"

"Kind of grayish green. Light wasn't too good."

"You must of got a good look at him," Whiskers growled.

The deputy looked as though his supper wasn't setting right—almost resentful, it seemed to Howlett. He sounded that way too when he said, "What color was his hair?"

It was distinctly odd the way they stood waiting, neither one of them breathing, not even batting an eyelash.

"Reminded me of corn silk," Howlett said, and was suddenly aware of a clock ticking somewhere. "I guess you know him," Howlett said, "so why not let me out of here? It ain't like them two was a pair of leading citizens."

"Ain't it?" Whiskers said, staring narrowly at Howlett's hands.

"A couple of counterfeiters?"

"Counterfeiters! My God," Vaguely said—"Cretch-Crispen! You poor yammerin' idjit, them two owned the biggest mine in this camp!"

Howlett said sickly, "But those banknotes he took off them . . . Hell I saw them myself. Two saddlebags crammed—"

"The Glorietta pay roll," Whiskers said, and shook his head.

TWO

HOWLETT stood a while glumly staring at the jailer after Vaguely took his departure. The fellow sat tipped back against the door to the office happily chomping on a cud of cut plug. He had the sawed-off Greener across his lap. Every three or four minutes, regular as clockwork, he would send a gob of tobacco juice splashing against the brass gaboon. Guy was no mountain man in spite of the whiskers. He was still young enough to enjoy showing off.

A little joy, Howlett thought, would be a good thing for himself about now. That Roman-nosed character must be laughing his tail off! Knowing very well the kind of bind he was in, Howlett still found himself occasionally prefacing a thought with *When that fellow gets back here tomorrow* ... knowing all the time that son of a buck wasn't coming back.

Howlett frowned, shaking his head. Though he had heard Vaguely's remarks on the subject, a corner of his mind kept advancing the somewhat preposterous feeling that, while Cretch and Crispen may have been the camp's biggest operators, they might also have been mixed up with that etcher. He was aware that greed or a too lively regard for the advantages of power could twist a man around to where his own friends couldn't account for his actions. Howlett had seen such things happen. He knew what weird deceptions a harried mind could fob off on a man, understood that his own was whistling into the dark, trying to put down its fright by clinging to the fabric of what probably would prove sheer invention, hoping to uncover some route by which, with a couple of those acts of God people talked about, he could some way haul himself out of this jackpot.

He would need at least one, he reckoned, even to get started. He growled, "Hesoos Creesto!" and took hold of the bars as though he would tear them right out of their sockets. All his good feeling about this country had vanished; he was oppressed by it now, by every facet of its prospect. That Cretch-Crispen pay roll would prove a pretty solid fact. Certainly it had disappeared. And all he was able to offer in discount of his connection was words. He could talk about that marshal and the "etcher" the fellow had gone off to catch till he was blue in the face without bettering his position by the width of one whisker.

Resolved to come to grips with his plight, he could admit there had probably never been any etcher and the currency he'd been shown had actually been the missing pay roll; but that his mind still used the term *probably* in evaluating these matters showed how strong an impression that bold-eyed son had made!

Turning around to find some place to sit down, he was startled to discover he wasn't alone in the cage. Another fellow was standing over against the far side. The pallid glow from a lantern hung from a rafter high above the jailer's head did little to dispel the gloom. But now that he was conscious of the man, Howlett could make him out well enough.

He saw a gambler's striped pants, black broken-tailed coat, the pale blur of wilted linen behind bright splashes of color that came from an embroidered vest. A limp string tie deepened smudges of shadow under the man's jaw, and a tall silk hat was rakishly set upon black curling hair that came across high-boned cheeks in a pair of luxuriant burnsides. The look of a fop did not extend to the man's eyes. They were a cold smoky black, reflecting just now a kind of sardonic humor like the grin that suddenly tugged his thin lips. "You can sit on the floor when you get tired of standing."

Howlett's glance swept the cage. The place was bare as the palm of his rope-callused hand. At no point did the bars touch the walls or come near enough for a prisoner to touch them. The bottom of the grille was bedded in the floor which looked like crushed and pounded *caliche*. The top, eight feet above Howlett's head, went into the rugged beams of the ceiling. These bars were further strengthened by a relay of crossbars brazed on at about the height of Howlett's belt.

There was nothing a man could get loose for a weapon, no place where even a bug could have hidden.

"One entrance, one exit," Howlett's companion said dryly, inclining a thumb at the door behind Whiskers. Howlett stared at the sheet-iron lining this side of it.

He looked around the cell. "What happens to a man's natural functions?"

The tall gambler meagerly showed his teeth. "Best not to have any between seven and seven. They're not harsh here, just careful."

"I suppose you're Dollarosa. Boarder, or just resting?"

"Had to plug a short sport. They're waiting to find out if they're going to have to plant him. Used to be able to call my shots—grew up on a cow ranch. Eyestrain, maybe."

"No friends?"

The man showed a tight smile. Gamblers, Howlett remembered, were in the same hole with gunfighters when it came to having friends. "Must be somebody."

"When a gambler's eyes start to go, or his nerve, he'd better be looking for another occupation." Dollarosa flexed his fingers, grinned wryly. "If the feller gets up, I'll be free to find out if I can still fork a saddle."

Howlett, bone weary, sat down on the chalky floor, scrounging his back up against the bars. "Jailer," he said, "is your boss doing anything about finding that guy?"

"Which guy is that?"

"One that shot Cretch and Crispen."

"Come off it, feller."

"You've got a description."

Whiskers grinned. "We got a man too."

"If you're going to hold me for it, charge me. You can't just—"

"That right?"

"Who'd object?" Dollarosa said. "I remember one feller they kept here for six months. Never did charge him. Vaguely's careful. If that Dutchman hadn't confessed to the killing, I expect old Boston would still be taking his meals here. Wonder what ever became of that joker?"

The jailer's eyes began to glitter. Dollarosa stifled an elaborate yawn. "How about lowering that wick a little, Hanley?"

Whiskers said, "You know the rules."

"You ought to break this feller in gradual. First time you had me here, I like to went off my rocker."

"If you want my notion he won't have far to go," Whiskers said. He got up and pulled off his shirt, vigorously scrubbing the hair on his chest with it. Then he chucked the wadded-up shirt at the wall. "By Gawd," he said to Dollarosa, "I don't see how you can stick that coat!"

"I thought it was common knowledge gamblers haven't anything but ice water inside them."

"Someday," Whiskers said, "I aim to find out." He shifted the chair around, still hanging onto his shotgun, resettled himself and tipped back against the door. He said, eyeing Howlett,

"What name do you go by?"

"Howlett."

"We got a circular on you?"

Howlett said, "No."

"You look like we ought to have."

"I've seen guys that looked like pillars of the church that would cut your throat for as little as ten cents."

"They're goin' to miss you, mister."

Howlett closed his eyes to get away from the glare.

"You sleep in that hat?"

"Mostly I wear it to keep the sun off my bald spot."

"Sun won't bother you here. Toss it out."

When Howlett gave no evidence of hearing, Dollarosa murmured, "I've a notion we'll both be a heap more comfortable if you try to get along with the help around here."

Without opening his eyes Howlett pulled off the hat and shoved it through the bars. Through the cracks of his lids he got a look at the jailer, discovering the expected interest with which the man was regarding the exposed streak of white hair.

"How'd you get that?"

"Mule," Howlett said, and let his eyes come fully open. He'd found only a natural curiosity in the jailer's look and voice, but there was certainly something peculiar in the way the man's eyes cut back to Howlett's hand. And Whiskers wouldn't be forgetting that streak. If anyone around here had heard of White Howlett, the law wouldn't be long in the dark about him.

Hanley said, "Yours too, Dollarosa."

The gambler smiled. "I'm surprised, with that shotgun, you'd be afraid of a hat." He took off his silk tile, sadly shaking his head, and tenderly dusted it with the back of a coatsleeve. Collapsing it, he said, "This bonnet set me back quite a piece of change." Like a hoop he rolled it between the bars of the grille.

It came to rest against one of the jailer's legs.

"Very neat," Whiskers said. "Feller could play some cute tricks with this thing. If that sucker kicks off—"

"Let's not hasten the poor man's demise by talking of it. If he should be so misfortunate, you may have it with my blessing."

Howlett closed his eyes, and out of sheer exhaustion, slept.

A sudden shout woke him. It was like so many of the shouts in his sleep that Howlett's hand dropped instinctively to grip the gun that wasn't there. Shock exploded through his eyes, which wildly mirrored the rows of bars and, skittering around, smashed into the gambler, growing wickedly grim with returning memory.

"The Blind Mule jail," Dollarosa murmured.

Beyond the grille a voice growled, "Rise an' shine you sorry bastards!"

The uncalled-for, querulous ill-tempered tone of it hauled Howlett's head about. "Day man,

Anvil Orso—"the gambler began, and was told to shut up.

Orso, Howlett saw, was an older, stringier, smaller breed of cat than the whiskered one who had kept the night's vigil. His eyes were as sharp as Hanley's, but lacked their tolerance. Howlett's experience warned him that this fellow was either a zealot or some crazy fanatic—the hallmarks were in those jerky mannerisms, the gangling limbs, the pinched, hungry look about the coarse-lipped mouth and nostrils.

The man clattered a key in the lock, yanked open the grating, stepped back with the Greener leveled. "C'mon—git out of there! An' no goddam tricks!"

Both men moved as though they were stepping over eggs onto a sheet of glare ice. When Orso bade the gambler open the iron-plated plank door into Vaguely's office, Dollarosa did so and stiffly awaited the man's further word before stepping through, Howlett gingerly following.

"You know the routine," Orso called from behind. "Don't add to it or take anything away without you're lookin' for a short route to hell." The hammers of the Greener were thumbed back to full cock. "Foller that Mexican; do what he does."

Howlett hoped the son of a bitch didn't stumble.

Following Dollarosa around to the back of the jail, he found egress blocked by a fence of rough plank seven feet tall, with the timbers stood up like pickets and held together by strands of barbed wire nailed in place on both sides. A rusty, short-handled, broken-bladed spade lay on gophered ground in the tiny courtyard made by this enclosure. The air was rank. Dollarosa stepped over by the fence and stood with his back turned.

The dry rasp of Orso's voice prodded Howlett. "Use that shovel if you're going to do anything needs buryin'. You got two an' a half minutes—better make up your mind."

Howlett choked back the anger that came up in him like bile.

Orso's lips curled. "Proud one, eh?" He spat across the barrels of the sawed-off Greener. "Ever see a man that's been swung with his gut full?" He snorted, shifted his weapon and stepped back against the wall. "Time's up. Get started, tinhorn."

Dollarosa, with his face like pounded putty, strode between them, heading for the alley mouth. Ignoring Orso, Howlett moved after him. The gambler turned left at the front of the jail, stepped up onto the walk that ran the full width of Kelly's and clomped to a stop without being told before the swing doors of the New York Cafe. Howlett, stopping beside him, saw Orso's shadow as the man came up. "All right. Go on in."

Once more Howlett trailed the gambler. A couple of miners in muck-discolored brogans held down stools at the far end of the barlike counter. They glanced around, looking curiously at Howlett, then went back to shoveling food into their faces. Howlett sat down beside Dollarosa. Orso pulled out a chair at a nearby table and sat back, cuddling the shotgun.

The place was steamy even at this hour, and stank of stale grease. A clatter of tableware came out of the kitchen. A sweating hasher appeared, sliding platters of ham and eggs in front of them, swiveling from the hips to pour two coffees, bending under the counter to come up with a brace of scorched, runty biscuits. "Five minutes," Orso grunted as the girl flustered off with her arms filled with dishes.

Both men buckled down to it. "Not Delmonico's," Dollarosa declared, "but at any rate filling." He picked up one of the biscuits. "Saleratus," he said through his chewing. "If Jim gives you the chance, you better dig for the tules."

Howlett, looking thoughtful, went on with his eating. Presently he said, "I've an idea both of them recognized that fellow."

"It won't do you any good."

"Let's go," Orso growled, getting up with the shotgun.

Neither of them had finished. Howlett, looking around into the muzzles of the Greener, got down off his stool and followed Dollarosa out. A swamper was sweeping off the walk in front of Kelly's; he stepped down into the dust to let them pass. A wind, springing up, flapped the tails of the gambler's coat. He said, "What's the word, Charlie?"

The swamper peered up at him dubiously. "No change."

"While there's life there's hope." Dollarosa smiled.

"You open that mouth again," Orso said, "I'm goin' to knock most of them teeth down your windpipe."

THREE

JIM Vaguely, the law at Blind Mule, was an honest man in a job which continually filled him with frustration. Time and again he had been forced to ignore the truth because he couldn't dig up enough proof for conviction. Upon other occasions, having what had looked to be conclusive evidence, he had been fouled up by plain and fancy lying. He could arrest drunks and drifters, run off a small-time crook or lock up a Dollarosa for a shooting he'd been forced into, but when it came to putting any crimp in the big stuff—the clubbings and killings that went on all the time—he was licked before he started. Everybody wanted a wide-open camp. Appeals to the sheriff got him nowhere at all. Political chicanery he could understand; it was public indifference that made a travesty of justice. A less stubborn man would have washed his hands of the whole sickening business.

He even had to be stuck with a jailer like Orso who wasn't more than one cross to being removed from a mad dog. None of Vaguely's philosophizing nor all his bitter disgust had been able to conjure a replacement—which made the blessing of a man like Hanley assume the proportions of what might be called a miracle. Whiskers had walked into Jim's office one day and coolly grinned him out from under a gun which had been obviously cocked for murder. After the drunken miner had been got out of there, the stranger had said he was looking for a job. It hadn't made sense then; it made even less now. Why any young robustuous galoot of his dimensions would be willing to sit under a jailhouse lantern when he could make twice the pay doing almost anything else in this camp was more than Jim Vaguely could understand. Hanley might be lazy but he sure as hell wasn't careless. It was him who had plated the back of that door.

The total uselessness of practically everything he'd done or tried to do in aid of justice had the harassed sheriff's deputy just about ready to give up on Blind Mule when Howlett had come in packing Cretch and Crispen. After locking Howlett up, Vaguely had spent upward of an hour thumbing old dodgers without turning up a thing. He'd used another thirty minutes going over the stranger's story, after which he'd gone out and done a prowl through the town.

There'd been a mounting excitement working through him, worriedly tempered by apprehension. This could be the break he'd been waiting for. He sent a man after the coroner and carefully weighed Old Doc's opinion before committing the pair of corpses to the icehouse. He was not expecting any marshal on the morrow, yet on the whole that yarn coincided quite dramatically with a number of notions which had lately been claiming no little of Vaguely's attention.

The deputy found himself nodding, halfway convinced in spite of the yarn's wilder aspects. If this fellow had made the whole thing up, he could certainly have done a better job for plausibility. If he'd killed Cretch and Crispen, he'd have taken that pay roll and lit a shuck out of here.

There were a couple of things about the man's story Vaguely could swallow without even chewing. That description for one! Howlett couldn't have described a man that closely without having seen him. Howlett's badge packer was Harry Rimrose; a rancher in whom Vaguely had recently developed quite an interest; circumspectly, of course. Rimrose was one of this region's largest operators, a power in the land, a rough man to lay hold of if he'd made up his mind to discount the rules. The only real doubt in Vaguely's head had to do with the rancher's intention.

Had Rimrose been caught redhanded by this stranger, or was the stranger part of something boldly rigged in the hope that Vaguely would stick his neck out? The deputy felt the prickle of sweat. The possibilities scared the hell out of him.

There was no question of these killings putting Rimrose in a spot where the law could make an example of him. Howlett was a stranger. He

wasn't right for the part of solid citizen's ac-
cuser. Rimrose would laugh, make fools of all of
them. A dozen men would swear he'd been getting their lights snuffed. There was no way
Vaguely could use what had happened, but there
was one thing he could do. He could bring them
together and perhaps discover to his own satisfaction where Rimrose stood. It could mean, if
the deputy were lucky, an end to his uncertainty,
a place to begin, a chink in the rancher's armor
which the law might one day find some means of
widening.

Vaguely, doggedly making his rounds, did a
deal of thinking without getting much further.
Knocking off his patrol of the camp about two,
he returned to his office to get what rest he
could. At six he got into his head and boots and,
with increasing perturbation, walked around to
the New York Café. He gulped down his food
without hunger or relish, the same sort of fare
the county's star boarders were served an hour
later. He soaked in the barber's tub, had a shave.
When he couldn't find anything else to kill time,
he got his horse and left town.

By nine the climbing blaze of the sun had gen-
erated about all the heat a man could comfortably take. He reckoned the day was going to
be a real scorcher. What the country needed was
a couple of days of rain. He checked his gun.
Fiddled with his holster. He was nervous as a cat
going across a tin roof.

At a little before ten he crested the last rise
and, with sweat making dark rings under both

armpits, considered the tactical simplicity of the ranch headquarters Rimrose had laid out at the head of Seven Mile Draw.

Everything about the place was strictly utilitarian. There were no clutters of scrap. The yard was as grimly bare as an army post; there wasn't a shrub or a tree within three hundred yards of the buildings. These were sod-roofed adobes. The ranch-house walls were two feet thick, their slotlike windows heavily shuttered. Six horses stood sleepily hipshot in the day corral, paired off nose to rump, tails occasionally swishing in discouragement of flies. All the rest of the pens were empty and set at some distance beyond the line of boxlike outbuildings. One of the geldings looked up and nickered. A man with his arms white with flour to the elbows stuck his face out of the cookshack.

"Boss around?" Vaguely hailed.

"Try the house."

With a prickling sensation between the blades of his shoulders, Vaguely, reining over to the porchless fort, gingerly got down. He knew it was silly to be nagged in this way. How could there be any grounds for apprehension? The rancher couldn't know what he had in his head. Even if he guessed, what difference? Rimrose had nothing to be worried about—he was a lion in this country; the law was a mouse.

"Anybody home?"

Letting go of the reins he went up and thumped on the door. For a moment there was nothing but silence, quiet like a blanket covering all with its muffling folds. Somewhere in the house a chair was shoved back. A rhythmic tramp of boots reached out to him dimly. A shape appeared where the door had been.

Rimrose, recognizing the law, turned still. Some of the cat look went out of his eyes. "Well . . ." He finally stepped back. "Come in, Jim."

"Quite a place you've got here."

Closing the door, Rimrose came after him. "Straight ahead," he said—"right through that arch. When you reckon we'll get any rain?"

The house seemed dim after the outside glare. The shutters were closed to keep out the heat. It was ten degrees cooler inside the thick walls. This huge room, Vaguely noticed, was comfortably furnished. He moved through the arch and took a chair against the wall. Here too were the same slotlike windows, but their barricades were open to let in the light. He sprawled back, letting weariness come out of him like sweat. Hands idle in his lap, he watched the rancher pour two drinks; then he took and held the one he was handed. Rimrose, having tossed off the other, sagged comfortably back in the chair behind his desk.

"Book work!" he grumbled, waving a hand at the open ledgers. One sharp line creased his forehead, remaining even when he smiled. "Pretty hot day to be pounding your rump."

"Pretty hot," Vaguely agreed, and stared down into the folds of his hands.

The rancher waited politely. Vaguely looked to have got lost in his thoughts. "Drink up,"

Rimrose said, skreaking around in his chair. "Plenty more where that come from."

"One'll do." Bending forward, the deputy put his glass down on the desk. "Guess you heard about Cretch and Crispen. Both of them shot dead."

"Heard you had the killer locked up."

"I got *some*body locked up. Like to have you take a look at him."

The sound of a clock crept through the room. The crease on Rimrose's forehead cut deeper. He pushed a box of hay-colored cigars across the desk and, the deputy passing, took one himself. "Why me!"

"You get around. This feller looks like a bad one, but I can't dig up anything on him. I thought—"

"What does he say?"

Bumbling, ineffectual, Vaguely looked like a man caught in circumstances too complex for him; like a bogged-down cow, a dreary picture of futility. Even the shake of his head held a kind of bovine dumbness. "That's the queerest part of the whole business." He repeated Howlett's story.

The lighted match the rancher was holding burned down. He looked startled and dropped it. "Do I understand you to think the description he gave of that supposed marshal fits *me?*"

The deputy shrugged. Abruptly he knew he'd been right to be worried. The ranchman's face was butter bland, but the stink of danger was all around, so real and close he could almost taste it. Fear closed his throat, and then he heard himself saying, "Take a look in your mirror," and was astonished at the casualness he had managed to put into it. "What I thought was perhaps you might have crossed tracks with him before. Nobody gets very far in this world without steppin' on someone."

Rimrose looked at him carefully. "I suppose that's so." He got out of his chair and picked up his hat.

It was close to four in the afternoon when Howlett dozing in a corner of the cell, heard the tramp of boots in the office back of Orso and saw the jailer get up as someone hammered on the door.

Orso clamped the shotgun against his hip and thumbed back both hammers. "What's the racket about?"

"Open up!" Jim Vaguely said.

Orso took his own good time. Still holding the Greener, he crabbed over to the door, scraped back the iron shield and peered through the slot. What he saw must have convinced him, but it didn't improve his temper. Unbarring the door he backed off, not bothering to open it, taking up a stand against the wall, the murderous weapon in his hands still cocked.

The deputy pushed the plank door open and came in, thoughtfully followed by a taller man. Howlett watched this one stand inscrutably silent, his expensive clothes faintly powdered with dust, yet in some way appearing to seem immaculately crisp in spite of the heat, which must have stood well over a hundred.

"Howlett, get up," the deputy said. "This is Harry Rimrose."

Rimrose shook his head. "Never saw him before."

Vaguely's hope was with Howlett.

"What is this?" Howlett said. "Some kind of game?"

"This is the man you told me about. The one you described as a Federal marshal."

"You must have been out of your head," Howlett said.

FOUR

ALL the while Jim Vaguely was eating, his thoughts continued to revolve around Rimrose and the desperation and violence to be found on every hand. No man was safe after dark who had money in his pockets or was rumored to have hidden any. The camp's main output was copper and, since this was not readily negotiated as ore, disputes over claims were not particularly troublesome; but road agentry thrived, brawls were so common as to pass almost unnoticed and murder was frequently committed in broad daylight. The big company mines were threatening to shut down if something wasn't soon managed to ensure the safety of payrolls. As one company spokesman angrily put it, "Every second son of a bitch you pass in this camp is either a robber or is tied in with robbers!"

Vaguely recalled the butter-smooth blandness of Rimrose's stare, the deadly quiet of that moment following the disclosure of Howlett's story. Superimposed upon these were the scene at the jailhouse, the consternation he had experienced when, as the deputy viewed it in his own mind, Howlett had let him down. He had been prepared for the rancher's disclaimer, but Howlett's repudiation had left him stranded in alarm and confusion; and yet it was not hard to guess what had been in Howlett's mind.

The man was a stranger, alone in a tough camp. One had only to look at Rimrose to feel the power and reach, the danger of his antagonism which formidably waited like the fangs of a rattler. His importance was evident in bold eyes and arrogant presence; the deadliness Vaguely had felt himself. Howlett was no fool. He would have taken in the costly clothes, the benchmade boots, the assuredness that came out of the man, adding these up to their inescapable total and setting beside it his effrontery and impudence, remembering the ruthless end of Cretch and Crispen hardly a stone's throw beyond camp limits.

No, Vaguely thought, you couldn't blame Howlett. Better to be stuck where he was, in jail, than to attempt any stand on so impossible a story. Better to be faced with public indignation, even imprisonment, than risk his life in an identification so palpably useless. The deputy realized this, yet it was hard for him to see any chance—however remote—thrown away when just possibly it might have made all the difference.

The time, though not yet, was surely approaching when these armed robberies and manhandlings must bring the whole region into open and bitter conflict. Men could be bullied and frightened and beaten, but there was a point whose crossing, beyond despair, would inevitably bring reprisals and retribution. It was for this that Jim Vaguely waited. Smart and slick as Rimrose had shown himself, the man's greed and brashness and contempt for intelligence in others would soon or late put him out in the open; and when that time came Jim meant to be here to see it. There was smoke, all right, and a little flame, but the heart of the fire was hard to get at.

Night came again and darked the boards for new transgressions.

Vaguely prowled the street, doubts creeping in to undermine his recent convictions, and he was no longer sure of anything. Howlett could have been lying, the story he'd fabricated a screen for intentions not yet apparent.

He thought some more about Rimrose. Even the danger he had sensed while they'd been talking at the ranch could have been contrived out of nothing more tenable than the frustrated anger too long bottled inside him. There was nothing to fasten onto without belief in Howlett's story but the high rung of the rancher's position and present standing on a county-wide basis. There was nothing wrong with being big—this was every man's dream when you came right down to it; the fruits of endeavor, of hard work, foresight and perseverance. The man gave to charity, had helped many a poor duffer down on his luck, had even put a few bad ones right into his crew on the chance that right living might reclaim them for better ends. And if there were those who didn't believe that ... What he needed, Vaguely felt, was to get farther back, nearer to the man's beginning, to what Rimrose had been before he'd got where he was—but who would you ask?

Vaguely's attempts to reminisce with old settlers had got him nowhere until he'd gone to the cow camps. The turn of his talk had there got him eyed with a frosty reserve as soon as the name of Rimrose came into it. The only definite thing he had discovered for sure was that the boss of Two Pole Pumpkin was not considered a favorable topic for discussion.

Back in his office, nursing a foul-smelling pipe, Vaguely was again rather bleakly working through that stack of lost men when the street door was flung open and as abruptly pushed shut. He stared with startled eyes at the girl backed against it. A whorl of smoke curling along the stem of his pipe ribboned upward against the push of cold air. Recalling his manners, he let go of the dodgers and got onto his feet. "Chair, Miss Frankie?"

"Where is he?" she said, coming straight to the point.

"If I knew ..."

"That fellow—the one who brought in Cretch and Crispen."

Vaguely was considerably put out with himself for not having thought of her sooner. Her dad, Eli Tappen, had last year been killed accidentally during roundup. He'd been handling the irons and was bent over, reaching to pick up a fresh one, when a wall-eyed cow, crazed by what was happening to her calf, had broken past the ropers and come straight for him. The man with the knife had let out a yell just as one of Rimrose's men—the only other one apparently who had noticed what was happening—jerked his pistol and threw down on the cow. The shot never touched her. Tappen alerted by the yell, had lunged whirling onto his feet and caught the slug between the eyes.

All of this the deputy had suddenly remembered, but the reason she interested him particularly now was that a part of her range abutted Two Pole Pumpkin. "I don't guess ..." he began, then asked instead, "What do you want with him?"

"I'd like to hire him if I can."

Vaguely tried to dissemble his astonishment. "Look," he said, "if you're short a hand ..."

"I know what I want!"

"Yes, ma'am."

"He hasn't left, has he?"

"He's around," the deputy said, "but—"

"Where is he?"

"I've got him locked up."

He couldn't tell what she was thinking, but the look of her made him acutely uncomfortable. He took the pipe out of his mouth, scowled, relit it, and put a cloud of smoke around him. Her eyes never moved. Lots of ways she was like her father; Tappen had been stubborn too. Vaguely said, half angry: "Story he give, a kid in three-cornered pants couldn't swallow. I don't know what you've heard, but Cretch and Crispen was tryin' this time to get that pay roll through theirselves. The facts is simple. The money's gone, Cretch and Crispen's dead, this stranger comes into camp packin'—"

"You surely can't believe he killed them himself!"

"Times like this I don't know what I believe. But I can tell you this—this feller's nobody you'd want in your outfit. Man can smell gunsmoke three blocks away from him!"

"I was on Tigley's porch when he rode past. I'll take my chances—"

"Chances! God of Golgotha! That feller's a *killer*, girl!"

"Yes," she said. "You can't fight fire with an empty bucket."

He stood there without enough breath left to cuss with. Heat came into his cheeks. "Hirin' fellers like that ain't—"

"Jim, I've got to do *some*thing."

He chewed at his cheek. "Been losin' cows, have you?"

"That's only part of it."

"If you got killin' trouble, Frankie, the law—"

She said, in exasperation: "There's nothing for the law to get hold of. You ought to know Rimrose by now. Ever since he came into this country he's been wild to get Star Cross—came to Dad twice trying to buy it. Last time he offered almost double what it's worth, cattle included.

"When was this?"

"Just before Dad was killed."

Vaguely took the pipe from his mouth. "He made any more offers?"

She shook her head. "Someone's stealing me blind."

"But I thought you and Rimrose. . ." Vaguely's face reddened. "I mean—"

"I know what you mean, I suppose," she said with a lift of her chin, "the whole country is talking about the way he has practically camped on my doorstep! I can't do anything with him."

"What about Bill Virgen? Ain't he still roddin' your spread?"

"Jim, I don't trust Bill. I know—it sounds crazy. But there is something mighty queer about a man who, in all the years he's been with Star Cross, has never said one single thing about his past."

"Nothin' so queer about that. You could say as much for half the fellers in this country. It ain't what a man's been but what he is that—"

"You ever look into Bill Virgen's eyes?"

"Lord God!" Vaguely said. "Women's notions! Your father hired him. He was about as good a judge—"

"I'm not so sure. There were a lot of things . . . It was more Tom's judgment than Dad's, I think, that built Star Cross into a big operation. It's never been quite the same since he quit—and there's another funny thing: Tom just up and quitting overnight and going off and Virgen turning up so pat like he did to step into Tom's boots." Her green eyes searched Jim's face. "You never knew Tom, or you would see what I mean. He never had a fiddlefooted thought in his life. Did you know Virgen showed up in this country just three months ahead of Rimrose?"

Vaguely said, somewhat disgruntled by the sound of it, "I ain't found out yet when Rimrose came into this."

"Five years ago—I keep forgetting you're new here. There wasn't any mining then; wasn't much of anything but Star Cross and maybe a dozen two-bit outfits squatting around through the hills wherever they could find water. That was the year of the big dry. He came in here riding a forty-dollar horse that looked like one good breath would knock it over."

"What kind of outfit did he have?"

"All he had was that horse and a dozen sorry cows. Six months later he not only had a crew but five hundred head of cattle and all the grass that had been supporting six of those greasy-sackers. By the end of that first year he'd doubled the range and tripled the herd."

The deputy swapped a long glance with her. "Night ridin'?"

"You couldn't prove it."

Vaguely stared for a while and then knocked out his pipe. Going over, he banged on the door of the jail. "Open up!"

After they had been to the café for their supper and were locked up again with Whiskers Hanley back in his chair against the wall with the Greener, Dollarosa sighed. "Nothing's changed. You saw him and he saw you. He ain't going to be forgetting it."

Howlett sat with arms loosely folded about his

knees. The only sign he gave of being different from a rock was when he hunched the bend of his spine a little, trying to give cramped shoulders some relief from the gouge of bars.

"You been dealt a poor hand. You can't pass," the gambler said, shifting around to see how he was taking it, "and—since he knows what you've got—you can't do any bluffing."

"Tough tit," Whiskers said, stifling a yawn as he shook his head.

"Can't you say *any*thing?" Dollarosa demanded.

"What do you want me to say?" Howlett showed a faint smile. "We've still got the draw. Might pick up something there."

Dollarosa looked as though the words came from an idiot. Whiskers Hanley chuckled. "From a stacked deck?" he asked skeptically.

"A stacked deck," Howlett said, "is something made by hands." He withdrew from the conversation by the simple expedient of closing his eyes.

A half-hour dragged by; another quarter trailed it drearily. It seemed to Hanley, thoughtfully watching, that Howlett had passed through an invisible wall. It was uncanny, considering the jam he was in, that a man could appear so utterly indifferent to what might be in store for him. It took a pretty hard character, the jailer thought, to do that.

Mostly what it took was long apprenticeship to trouble. Out of past experience Howlett had learned to rest when he was able. He said into the settled fabric of that quiet: "Man's got two ways of getting around. He can use his feet like the rest of the herd or use what brains the good Lord has given him."

Whiskers said, "Your feet ain't goin' to walk through them bars."

Howlett's eyes stayed shut. He seemed to have gone off again. The gambler stood like a man dripped from wax. He didn't say anything either. Hanley, renewing his grip on the Greener, watched them both with an unwinking stare.

Howlett was remembering the girl who'd turned to peer at him from the porch of Tigley's store, feeling again those unwanted emotions, recalling what he had seen of her face. She had been too intent, too completely absorbed, for her interest to have stemmed from idle curiosity. In back of the wonder and worry he was sure of, there'd been something, he thought, which had been very like fright. He put her out of his mind. A man with his record had no right to think of women. Not decent ones.

Muted fragments of sound hauled his eyes out of hiding. Dollarosa, wholly still now, was inscrutably watching the door. Howlett nodded. There was somebody in the office. Even before he heard Vaguely's fist, he knew it would be the girl.

Hanley let them in.

Howlett was sure when she stood before him that his first impression had been correct. She was decent, and complexly filled with contradictions. Young—in her twenties probably. A quail-colored dress fitted tightly at neck, shoulders and waist. It was her face that caught his interest, the ridges of bone he had noticed before making the overlay of skin a screen for light and shadow, for fractional glimpses of thought as elusive as quicksilver. Her lips were full and curving and red across a face made compellingly vivid by a capacity for feeling which sometimes, he thought, must be the worst kind of torture. Her eyes were the green of new cottonwood leaves, brightly clear, long-lashed and disturbing, calling afresh in him the remembered hungers they had loosed before.

He was suddenly conscious of the sweat-soaked shirt damply clinging to his shoulders, and pulled his eyes away to find Jim Vaguely oddly watching. Continuing to regard him with jaundiced speculation, the deputy brusquely ordered Howlett onto his feet. "Let him out," he told Hanley. Whiskers unlocked the cage and, when the Texan stepped past him, clanged the grille shut.

Vaguely extended the confiscated hat, but Howlett said coolly, "I'm not going anywhere."

The sheriff's deputy accorded the remark no visible notice. "This," he said, "is Frances Tappen. Miss Frankie proposes I parole you in her care."

"I'm satisfied right here."

Vaguely's stare held an obscure edge. "Nobody asked for your opinion."

"Isn't this a little highhanded?"

"You want a hemp necktie? Those miners are pretty stirred up," Vaguely said. "Three of the mines have shut down. With time on their hands, and plenty of rotgut, it wouldn't take much—"

"It would take dynamite to crack this jail."

"They've got plenty of that, too," Whiskers said.

Howlett said, wooden-faced, "What am I charged with?"

"Haven't put any charge against you. You're bein' held as a material witness." It was plain the deputy was trying hard to hang onto his temper. "Look, man," he said, "I'm tryin' to do you a favor. This is only for just a little while. What's so rough about working for Star Cross?"

"If it wasn't rough, if she was just hunting a saddle hand, she wouldn't be coming around here."

"That's right," the girl said. "You might as well know the truth. Star Cross is the largest ranch in the basin—"

"Sorry," Howlett said. "I wouldn't be comfortable working for a woman."

He saw the bright color flare into her cheeks, saw them whiten.

Vaguely said, sounding disgusted, "Miss Frankie's in a bind—"

"She has my sympathy."

"It ain't sympathy she wants; it's help—"

"Then why don't you get out and start earning your stipend?"

Vaguely's affronted stare skewered Howlett. "You think I wouldn't if my hands wasn't tied? I got to have proof, and she ain't able to get none. But she's satisfied in her own mind—"

"Did you ever know a woman that wasn't?"

"By God," Vaguely said, "her trouble's Rimrose!"

Howlett, braced to resist any kind of appeal but that one, found his glance going back to the girl. She looked as much out of place in the role of big rancher as a cow would in bloomers. She was standing there awkwardly, hands creasing and recreasing one of the pleats in her skirt.

He looked her over hard while he was at it, knowing his scrutiny embarrassed her. It came to him suddenly that she was inordinately shy, and probably as conscious of the poor figure she cut as she was of his maleness and of her own lack of look. She was biting her lips now, her cheeks flaming painfully. But she wouldn't take her eyes away; and somehow, abruptly, this was mighty important. He called himself seven kinds of a fool, but he knew, because of Rimrose, he was going to wind up doing what she wanted.

FIVE

"WE'LL be holding the inquest," Vaguely said, "soon as the coroner gets in from Bloosom— probably sometime tomorrow. I'll let you know."

Howlett, saying nothing, followed the girl out into the office. She had the stride of a man, and this, unaccountably, irritated the hell out of him. She hadn't been much around women. They'd have made her do something about her hair— about that straddle-house red she had smeared like a goddam chippy across her mouth. Woman grown, and not knowing the first thing about how to be one! He couldn't help eyeing the dress. Good material and well enough cut, but a buffalo bull would have looked more at home in it. He couldn't see how she figured to get on a horse without hiking the damned thing up to her navel.

She turned around then and caught the slanch of his stare. Going painfully red she said, "I—I came in a buggy . . ." and saw the outraged look of him. She could not know the only "buggy bosses" Howlett had got near enough to shoot at

had been second-generation carpetbaggers. "I—
I'm sorry," she stammered, appalled and miserable at having once again offended him.

Vaguely, coming up behind them, said,
"You'll find your horse at the Good Oats livery
—I'll take care of the bill." He bent over his
desk, pulling open a drawer. "I've had your
hogleg and shell belt here for safekeeping." He
reached the steel and leather out to him. "Better
strap them on."

"You and your soft job!" Howlett growled
and, leaving them rolled, tucked them under an
arm. "I'm ready whenever you are, ma'am."

He followed her out and helped her into the
buggy.

"The Good Oats," she said, "is in the next
block. I'll wait for you here."

It had been hot in the jail, but the cool crisp-
ness of that night at this high altitude made him
glad of his long handles. He had enough sweat
still on him to feel the nip in this rarefied air.

The street wasn't as congested as it had been
last evening, but quite a few men were still tramping the walks and the saloons looked crowded
with laid-off miners. He didn't see any ore wagons and only three big hats, all at some distance
across the ankle-deep dust of the hoof-pocked
road.

At the livery the man on duty, after the
Texan's explanations, fetched Howlett's blanket
roll. By the time he returned with Howlett's
buckskin in tow, the Texan had got into his

brush jacket and had the rest of his gear ready to tie back of the cantle. This he took care of, then stepped into the saddle.

The Bucket of Suds and Tom Kelly's place still appeared to be doing a good deal of business. The near part of the road was dappled with their lights, but the buildings across from them —a barbershop, harness store and a dry-goods establishment competing with Tigley's—were now dark, the passages between them black pools of impenetrable shadow.

The girl had got into some kind of coat, and the deputy was standing at the buggy step, talking. In parting he said, just as Howlett came up,"—a stone that will make men stumble, a rock that'll make them fall." He lifted a hand and, turning, said, "Good luck to you, friend," and went back to his office.

As she saw Howlett peer narrowly after the man, she lifted the robe off her knees, holding an end up invitingly. "There are things to be said; if you'll drive we can talk. . . ."

She saw the frown cross his face as his head tipped around, observed the obvious reluctance with which he caught up the buckskin's reins and slowly knotted them. He stopped to tug the girths and run a practiced hand between the fishcord cinch and the animal's belly. He threw another look toward the jail and at last came on. His left hand reached to take hold of the dash, when three big-hatted men moved out of the gloom of an alley. Howlett's eyes narrowed. He stepped back, silently watching as the three, competently mounted, fanned out and came up, neatly boxing him.

"Evening, Miss Frankie," Rimrose said, touching his hat but never for a moment taking his eyes off the Texan. "Kind of queer company for you to be keeping." He looked at her then, bold eyes going over her in open disapproval. "Ain't this the feller that killed Cretch and Crispen?"

Frances Tappen said coolly, "I didn't get that impression from my talk with Jim Vaguely—"

"It's the word that's going around town," Rimrose stated. "Some of those miners are pretty stirred up."

"I don't suppose you had anything to do with that."

Rimrose's expression became extremely thoughtful. "Sometimes I just don't know what to make of you." He considered her a moment, broad chest tipped forward, settling his weight against the forks of the saddle. He shook his head, smiling down at her. "A strictly generous impulse has let more people in for grief than you'd imagine. You're figuring to sign this drifter on or that old fool Vaguely would never have found enough nerve to turn him loose. Don't do it, Frankie. The feller's no good. If he's got any sense, he'll get back in that jail before somebody shoots him."

The girl asked, "Is that a threat?"

"Call it good advice. I wouldn't want to see

you getting in over your ears making yourself responsible for—"

"You have an interest in Star Cross, Rimrose?"

Howlett's voice, cutting through the man's words, pulled Rimrose's face around. "I've an interest in Miss Frankie—"

"Don't let it run away with your judgment." The cold contempt in Howlett's drawl scraped a sparkle of rage through the rancher's stare.

"What concern is that of yours?"

"You could probably find out if you want to push it far enough."

Rimrose's eyes turned black with fury. His pair of riders, flanking Howlett, came up into their stirrups, hands swinging toward hips. The girl's alarm hauled her onto her feet. "No," she cried—"no!"

Howlett's laugh was short. "It won't get beyond talk, don't worry."

For a long and trembling instant Rimrose sat tipped forward in the saddle, eyes watching Howlett with a terrible intensity. His two riders were ready to back his play; there wasn't a chance of this brash drifter coming out on top once the guns started spitting. Dead—that was how he wanted this bastard, and the wish burned wickedly out of his stare. The lift of a hand, one glance, would take care of it.

The girl, legs trembling, saw this too. Yet Rimrose held there, still. There was nothing in Howlett's look that would explain this unless it were that half-jeering indifference. Rimrose had been filled with fury, all the long-concealed viciousness straining in his face. He was a man who had never tolerated opposition, yet something was holding him back.

Rimrose drew a ragged breath. He wasn't afraid of this galoot; he had never seen the day when he had been afraid of anyone. Too much was at stake. He had contrived this only to scare the man—get his wind up. If he could get this drifter running, public opinion would do the rest. This wasn't the place or time to burn powder. He forced a smile, dropping back in the saddle, shifting his glance back around to the girl. "That's right," he said brusquely. "No skin off my nose what he does or what happens to him. It's you I was thinking of, your place in this community . . . all the good will Star Cross has built up which would surely be jeopardized if you start taking saddle tramps—"

"Let me worry about that!" Coming out of the shock of her scare, Frances Tappen said angrily: "I'm running Star Cross! I intend to keep on running it in spite of any notions you may have to the contrary!"

"Frankie, Frankie. . ." Rimrose shook his head at her. "Running a ranch is no job for a woman. A woman's place is in the home—"

"With a lapful of babies! Go on—say it!"

"Well, yes . . . now that you mention it. Babies, certainly. Taking care of the home, looking after some man. Those are the things that should come first with a woman." Rimrose looked at her sadly. "At least let me find you a man who can—"

"You needn't concern yourself," Frances said. "I've got a man."

Her cheeks were filled with the high color of embarrassed self-consciousness, but her chin was up. He read defiance in her stare.

"A jailbird! Frances, this town will crucify you."

A small desperate smile crossed the smeared red of her lips. "He won't be easily pushed around. If you have any friends handling Star Cross beef, I think you'd better advise them to get into some other line." She sat down, ignoring him, and pulled up the robe. Howlett, stepping in from the other side, unwrapped the reins.

Rimrose stared with an ugly wonder. "That's rough country out there. Better ask yourself what's in this for you, friend." The girl's eyes, enormously anxious and searching, pried at the inscrutability of Howlett's face. The others were watching Howlett, too. "You," Rimrose said, bringing his horse up beside him, "are headed for trouble."

Howlett smiled. "That cuts both ways. And I can tell you something else. There's only one other thing at Star Cross you'll ever get."

The rancher's eyes were too closely guarded to be read. He said, "What's that?"

"You'll know if I see you out there." Howlett shook up the reins and the horse started off.

Rimrose yelled after him, "Stay out of my way!"

Though Frances had told him there was much to be discussed, she seemed content to ride without opening her mouth. Near one o'clock, with something more than six miles by his reckoning behind them, Howlett said abruptly, "Better fill me in."

She looked around with a kind of shiver, then sat very straight, staring drearily into the moon-bathed blue and silver of the mile on mile of range stretching ahead of them. He guessed that she was in conflict, probably still going over that exchange with Rimrose, frightened now perhaps by what she had done, by the madness which had brought within the narrow confines of this buggy the total stranger she'd recruited from the Blind Mule jail. She'd been desperate, of course, but now she was doubtless giving herself fits, caught up in the possible consequences of her brashness.

She said, stiffly, "You can ride out of this if you want to."

"Suppose you tell me what it's all about."

She was silent so long he began to wonder if she'd heard him. At last she said: "That's one of the things that makes it so hard—there's really nothing a person can get hold of. Nothing provable, I mean. We've been losing stock. Rimrose has always wanted this place; he tried twice to buy it while Dad was alive." She told about the roundup, how Tappan had been killed.

"What sort of offer did Rimrose make?"

"Eighty thousand the last time, cattle included."

Howlett presently said thoughtfully, "Where would he get it?" She stared down at the hands tightly folded in her lap. She was tight inside, apprehensive and nervous as a high-strung filly. "I don't suppose," he said, "you remember your mother."

The green eyes came obliquely up, darkly astonished. "No," she said, and looked quickly away, self-consciously poking at her hair.

Howlett became aware of the rather cramped dimensions of the buggy seat. As though having just made the same discovery, his companion stampeded breathlessly into speech. She appeared to be talking off the top of her head, touching nothing of consequence, flittering about like a moth in a lamp's light, jumbling childhood recollections, the names of people who had no meaning for Howlett, side excursions into the vastness of the country. Out of this avalanche of words certain impressions began to take shape at the back of Howlett's mind; he began to see her in terms of a personality thrown back on itself at an impressionable age in a world of animals and uncommunicative men.

As her embarrassment wore away she became more animated. She grew eloquent in picturing the vast silences, the harsh realities of a child's existence where the spirit had no sustenance beyond imagination, no companion to cushion the shocks of growing up. There was no sign of self-pity. She hadn't been sufficiently conscious of her plight to sense that these experiences were not common. Her voice gradually dropped and took on an attraction which was almost like music, weaving a spell which took Howlett's thinking through unexplored vistas of new, enticing country. Caught up in the web of those melodious cadences, he was weirdly reminded of the neglected girl in the fable who, at the lift of a wand, became the belle of the ball. It was like a first glimpse from the top of a hill, as though each of them had stepped like some gorgeous butterfly out of the husk of a discarded past. It was beautiful but futile. Howlett would not be stepping out of anything.

He grew aware of the stillness. The horse had stopped and was cropping the sparse stubble that meagerly showed through drifted sand. Howlett didn't know how long the pair of them had sat there eyeing each other. Her face was filled with embarrassment again. Her hands were folding and refolding a bit of the robe that lay over her knees.

He said, gruffly, "Let's hear some more about Rimrose," and slapped the horse into movement, sending him along marks where wheels had previously climbed through the shale of the slope.

Stiffly at first, and then with more feeling, Frances recounted the man's arrival with a

handful of sorry travel-gaunted cows, of the
phenomenal growth of his ranch and brand
upon range formerly held by a number of others.

"What happened to those people?" Howlett
asked.

"I don't know. There was talk . . . I really
don't know. Perley Adams was one of them—he
owned Two Bars. Runs the Good Oats now."

"Sure you're losing stock?"

"Bill Virgen won't right out and admit it, but
I've—"

"Who's Virgen?"

"He's the Star Cross ramrod."

"Satisfied with him?"

"I think . . ." she began, but that brief hesita-
tion told him more than any words she could
have spoken.

"What about your crew? You reckon they've
had a hand in it?"

She appeared to be giving the question careful
consideration. "In my father's time we never had
less than twelve riders on the pay roll; right now
we've got six. Two of these Bill managed to hire
last winter. He hasn't been able to—"

"What happened to the rest of them?"

"One Bill fired. Two others were shot—it was
after this that Bill fired Otis. Otis was straw boss;
Bill seemed to think he'd had something to do
with those shootings. This," she explained, "was
in the first several months after Dad was killed.
Then along in the fall one of our boys was gored
—he was dead when Bill found him. Three

months later Curly Peterson was thrown and dragged by a horse he'd been riding for more than two years. The rest drew their time and rode out of the country."

"All but the four who are still toughing it out with you. And Bill Virgen can't be sure you've had losses," Howlett said softly. "What do your tallies show?"

"About the same." Frances shrugged. "No particular shrinkage that couldn't be accounted for by numbers probably missed through a short-handed gather."

Howlett looked at her sharply. "You mean in country like this each spread throws its own roundup?"

"Star Cross has. For the last couple of years." She said, after a moment, "I'm afraid I don't understand all I know about it." The rasp and skreak of the buggy wheels and the footfalls of the laboring horse bridged the following silence while Howlett's eyes grimly considered the terrain. "You've got to realize," she said stiffly, "that this ranch has been given a pretty hard name."

"How long has Virgen been with you?"

"Ever since Tom quit." She gave him the rundown on Tom, their previous foreman, covering much the same ground she'd gone over with Vaguely. "Dad never asked any questions; he stood looking at Virgen for perhaps half a minute, then gave him the job. Just like that." She said, after another small silence, "Three months later Harry Rimrose showed up and moved onto Box 7."

"Moved onto it how?"

"It was generally understood he'd hired grazing rights—I told you," she reminded him, "none of this could be proved. Old Man Mearchum saddled up one day and went off through the hills and never came back. His Box 7 spread was the start of Two Pole Pumpkin."

Howlett, watching the horse, shook his head. "I sort of got the idea, back there, Rimrose had kind of taken you under his wing. You want to tell me about that?"

"He's worked powerfully hard at putting over that impression. I suppose," she said bitterly, "everyone thinks we've had an understanding." Color came more darkly into her cheeks and she went on: "I let him call on me once, and he's been at it ever since. I doesn't make any difference whether I see him or not. He comes three nights a week. He sits out there on the porch with nothing showing through the creepers but the fire on his cigars—even the crew is beginning to believe it!"

They were on the top of a ridge now, rolling along a level where the spiny growths of prickly pear, wolf's candle and cholla were profusely abundant, topped now and again by the lofty shape of a lonely saguaro. There was also an occasional clump of Mormon sage, and there were lights in the distance where a clutch of buildings darkly huddled perhaps three-quarters of a mile

this side of some round-topped foothills. Be-
,tween these hills and the buggy was a platterlike
oval cram-packed with grass and stretching out
on either hand for a good many miles.

"Star Cross," Frances said. For a moment
Howlett looked as though he couldn't take it in.
Then he pursed his lips in a soundless whistle.
"No wonder Rimrose wants it! Enough grass
out there to feed ten thousand head." He said,
"Where's Two Pole Pumpkin?"

"Off beyond those hills."

"He got grass like that?"

She shook the red bun of her pulled-back hair.
"Not like that. Most of his range is in what we
used to call The Roughs—all up-and-down
country crisscrossed with cliffs and washes. In
dry weather it's like an inferno. It's been pretty
dry these past fourteen months. He doesn't lack
for water, but the way it's situated his cattle walk
off half their weight going back and forth to get
it."

"How does he get to town from his place?"

"He uses this road mostly. There's another
way around through the hills, but it's not too
good and it's eight miles longer."

Rimrose, Howlett reckoned, would burn every time he went over this road, and a man could
hardly blame him. The contrast between his
place and what she had was enough to turn his
kind half crazy.

Howlett, staring around him as they moved
down into that sea of grass, got to thinking

about the $80,000 Rimrose had offered her father. A pile of money, even if pieced out with Star Cross cattle. Still, the man could affort it if that business of Cretch and Crispen was any criterion. A man as bold as that wouldn't have any problem finding cash to swing a deal. But he wouldn't offer cash again. He had the girl backed into a corner; Howlett's presence in the buggy was the mark of her desperation. One by one Rimrose had closed most of the avenues by which she stood any chance of keeping her inheritance away from him. By Rimrose's figuring he just about had Star Cross in his pocket; all he had to do now to make it legal was marry her. She'd been smart enough to see that.

Howlett shook up the horse. "What's been keeping the grass so green down here?"

"We've got a lot of springs, for one thing. Dad always imagined we were sitting on top of an underground lake."

It could be. Most of the run-off from these hills and roundabout mountains would find its way into this basin. Her old man had chosen well when he had put his roots into this place. "Expect you've been having considerable trouble with Harry's cattle."

"We wintered a thousand head," she said grimly. "There's probably twice that many eating into it now. Cattle will be cattle, he says."

"You ever think of putting up a fence?"

"I'm not like to do any more than think. Every outfit in this country would blow up if we tried that. Besides, I don't have anywhere near enough cash."

"There are banks."

"Not for a woman. Not for anyone who has Harry Rimrose breathing down his neck."

"What you need," Howlett said, "is an army. One man isn't going to scare Harry off."

"The right man might."

Howlett's glance found her watching him. Moonlight crossed the angle of her jaw, the buggy top putting the rest of her face in shadow. He peered ahead again, irritably. There was a combination of things in this girl that disturbed and oppressed him, at the same time feeding the flame of a hunger he could not understand. "I'm not that man," he said shortly.

"Then I'm being an awful fool," she said, "for I'm giving you Star Cross, lock, stock and barrel."

SIX

HOWLETT stopped the horse. "Are you loco?"

She could see he was angry, not disposed to believe her. Behind these unmistakable facts something wild and black, filled with the snarl of an intolerant savagery, was stirring up a whole chain of reactions she had neither anticipated nor was able to grasp.

She'd been caught in uncertainty and tumult. Sight of his agitation calmed her. "I'm trying," she said, "to recognize the truth, and the truth of Star Cross is that I've already lost it. None of us own more than the handful of acres where we've set up headquarters. Whatever else we claim is ours only so long as we are able to hold—"

"I won't have it!" he said flatly. "I don't want your damned ranch!"

Watching the thrust of his face in the moonlight, discovering its tensions, the little wiry muscles that strain and outrage had heightened, seeing the whole rebellious aspect of the man, she knew the unsteadying intoxication of relief. She'd taken a long-odds gamble and saw now some prospect of bringing it off. Had he shown

less antagonism she might have gone on ques-
tioning the wisdom of what she had done; his
anger vindicated her belief in its rightness.
Rimrose had to be stopped. Howlett might never
forgive her, but she had what she wanted—a
club to fight back with.

She said: "It's already yours. While you were
getting your horse and possibles, I started a man
for the county seat. When they open the
recorder's office in the morning, a quitclaim carrying my signature will be filed. No matter what
you decide to do about it, you are going to be on
record as the owner of Star Cross."

"You little fool!" he snarled, and hauled back
an arm as though he would strike her. But he let
the arm fall, too filled with his fury to get out
another word. He snatched up the reins and
made a grab for the buggy whip, yanking the
horse half around in the shafts. But once more
something stopped him. Swearing, he rammed
the whip back in its socket. Glaring stonily at the
wink of lights, he sent the animal on.

Frances wisely kept still. He made a tough-
looking customer, forearms braced across
spread knees, holding the reins in his big-
knuckled hands. She could feel the lashing gusts
of his temper swirling like storm winds. She
gripped the seat tightly, glorying in this, not at
all afraid of him, hugging the exciting conviction
to her that here at least was one who would not
feel Harry Rimrose's wishes had come straight
down from Moses.

The lights of the ranch drew nearer. She could

glimpse the tall shapes of cottonwoods coming out of the mesmeric haze of blue shadows and the ancient mesquite which had been four foot thick when her father had come here. . . . *His* tree now! she was reminded in sudden panic. For a terrifying instant all the world tipped and quivered in a rush of nostalgic memories; but she threw up her chin, pulling great breaths deep into her, finding reassurance in the hard look of the Texan's profile. Lord—he'd already said he didn't want her damned ranch! He would do the right thing. . . . She had to believe that. Her bridges were burned.

Howlett's voice impatiently dragged at her. "What are you figuring to say about me?"

"What do you want me to say?"

He looked at her blackly. "If I had my wants I wouldn't be here."

"Sell out then and go—"

"By God, I've a mind to!"

They glared at each other. But he didn't say any of the things she could sense were bursting to be let out of him. He gave her another black stare and put his eyes on the road. "You keep that place lit up all the time?"

And now a new unease laid hold of her. "No," she said, just above a whisper. Night's coldness crept through the folds of her jacket. It must be close onto two o'clock. . . .

"They'll find out soon enough what you've done—don't go blurting it out when we get there. I've got to feel my way around"—he scowled—"give this Virgen a chance to tip his hand. Not like to be much love lost anyway, you fetching me in here over his head. Better tell him I'm strayman."

She was desperately listening to the wheels and the thudding clop of hoofs, trying to shut out the picture of Virgen's snake-cold eyes staring her father into giving him Tom's job.

"You hear?" Howlett said.

She bobbed her head, afraid to speak lest chattering teeth tell how frail was her courage, how towering her fright.

"You think that bugger's going to like having a man around who was hired over his head without his being consulted?"

She shook her head so vigorously some of the hair got loose and came down around her face like witches' bridles. His eyes were studying her suspiciously. "What's the matter with you?"

She had both hands up, trying to gather the flying strands back into their accustomed anchorage. "N-nothing," she said through a mouthful of pins. "You better watch him, is all."

His eyes were still probing. "I'll watch him."

He removed his regard to peer toward the ranch. She could see the buildings quite plainly now, the dark huddle of men grouped before the porch. Howlett sent the horse plopping into the yard; she felt the lurch as they went over the planks that bridged the ditch which carried the tank's runoff to the flowers she'd been trying to get to grow beside the house. She felt the banked stare of all those watching men, saw Virgen's burly shape come away from the crew as

Howlett brought the buggy to a stop.

"Where the hell you been?"

"Town," Frances said, holding tight to the seat.

"Next time you figure to pull a stunt like that, take somebody with you! We was just about fixin' to turn this country upside down. You don't know what kinda riffraff is prowlin' these hills."

Brittle anger was in his tone. She found no indication this had sprung from any concern over her, though she did think to catch an edge of harrassment running through it, a disquietude she could not understand. Wondering if he'd found out about Lippy going with her, she said, bolstered by Howlett's proximity, "I'll thank you to remember who you're talking to, Virgen."

There was patronizing mockery in the foreman's lifted stare. "I'll remember first of all you're a female an' damn near helpless." An emerald flashed as he rolled the flats of both hands along his hips in lazy circles. "We don't want to have to be hanging anybody."

She looked at the beefy slants of his shoulders, some of the hard-won defiance falling out of her. Virgen laughed. "You wouldn't want nothin' like that to happen." The dark whip of his glance came around to find Howlett. "What's this you've lugged home?"

"He's going to work as strayman—"

"Country's got all the strays it can use." A heavy cropped mustache hid Virgen's mouth; there was no doubt whatever about the look in his eyes. "Git aboard that nag, an' drift!"

Like a tired old man Howlett secured the reins to the whipstock. Unshaved and half in shadow he knew the poor figure he cut before these men. Maybe he was seeing a chance to slide out. He swallowed a couple of times and said dubiously, "I been hired—"

"Not by me. Any hirin' that's done around here, I do it."

"I gave him the job," Frances said. "His name's Howlett . . ."

"I don't care about that. He's not lightin' here!" The emerald flashed again as Virgen stepped around to Howlett's side of the rig. One hand shot up and got a hold on the arm rest at the side of the seat, the new man cringing back as Virgen's tug tore it loose. "I never tell any gazebo more than once." With bare hands he tied the cold iron in a knot and, watching Howlett maliciously, pitched it aside. A gold-capped tooth showed through his ugly grin as he fastened one of those grub-hooks into the front of Howlett's jacket. "Once is generally enough," he said, and tugged.

Howlett should have gone crashing into the ground face first, leaving little thereafter to be done but get him loaded. But somewhere between that tug and the dust boil something went wrong with Virgen's calculations. Breath burst out of the astonished crew when it became apparent it was the boss man himself staggering up off the ground. Howlett was six feet away, indolently lounging against the hub of a buggy wheel.

Virgen licked grit from his teeth.

The new man said casually, "Been having a little roll?"

The ramrod's eyes went narrow, expressionless as a cat's. He was obviously badly shaken. One side of his jaw was darkly abraded, the blood, clotted with dust, forming a kind of black paste. What had suffered most was his ego; and he was going to have to go through with this or lose all control of the Star Cross crew.

Howlett, straightening, came away from the buggy. He didn't reckon any offer of peace was going to help much, things being the way they were, but he said, out of his memories of Texas: "I never did figure much of anything gets changed by two rannies pounding the stuffing out of each other. The both of us is bound to be wanting what is best for Miss Frankie. I'm willing to—"

He gave up right then, twisting aside just enough to clear the ramrod's murderous fist-flailing charge. Nothing short of brute force, Howlett saw, would ever change the man's mind or intentions. So, as the fellow plowed past, Howlett brought the edge of a stiffened palm wickedly against the exposed side of Virgen's neck.

The ramrod piled up like a forefooted steer.

Dust thickened around him, boiling up through the shadow dappled light from the lamps. He came out of this haze like a prodded bull, breathing hard, fists balled, head jutting like a sidewinder's. This time Howlett didn't attempt to get away from him. He stood his ground until the man was practically onto him, dropping as Virgen's fists slammed toward him, then drove into the man's legs and upended him over a shoulder.

Virgen came out of this fall badly winded. The whole front of his shirt was in tatters and he limped badly. His gold tooth gleamed through the snag of scraped lips; but his eyes, though still wild, held a grudging caution. Bullheaded and ringy as he undoubtedly was, the man was no fool. He dredged up a parched grin. "You'll do." he said gustily. "Put your stuff in the bunkshack." He scrubbed an arm across his cheeks. "Baines, take care of them horses." He waved the rest of them away.

The girl got out of the buggy and, with a white look, went into the house. Baines, a spare, wiry shape in a pinto vest, stepped into the buggy and drove off toward the barn.

"I'll make out to tend at my own horse," Howlett said, wheeling around to start after him.

"Just a minute," Virgen said. "I've put you on, but that don't have to be the end of it."

Howlett twisted his head, looking over a shoulder. "Make it plain."

"You been goddam lucky. Don't be gettin' any notions. Long as you're drawing Star Cross pay you'll take my orders—"

Howlett, after giving him prolonged attention, saw no use in beating around any bushes. "Might's well get this straight right now. Any orders I take won't be relayed from Rimrose. Or," he said quietly, "hatched up to benefit him."

Shock, for about ten seconds, held Virgen; then his wheels started grinding. He put on a look of injured innocence, but he must have seen this was not going over and dropped the pretense, shifting his weight with solemn care. The planes of his cheeks showed darker; then he laughed it off and went limping away.

At the barn Howlett found Baines feeding the buggy horse; he had the animal in the last of a long row of four-by-ten stalls. The place was familiar with smells of hay and urine and accumulated dust. Everything here was in a clutter of neglect, and ancient droppings were all over the planks. No other horses were being held in the building.

Howlett stripped off the saddle and took the buckskin out on the reins to let him roll. Then he permitted him to drink from the moss-greened trough and was taking him back when Baines stepped out.

"You'll find oats in the bin again' the back wall."

Howlett jerked a brief nod and went on. The man was still by the door when Howlett returned. He held out Durham and papers. Howlett, gravely accepting them, put together a smoke, licked and lit it. "Something on your mind?"

Baines stared off across the yard. "First time anything like that ever happened." He let the silence pile up, scraping the toe of a boot against the ground. "Figgered you might like to know." He tucked the makings into his vest and drifted off in the direction of the bunkhouse.

Howlett stood for a few moments squinting into the dark. He sighed heavily then and ground out his smoke. Shouldering his blankets and single spare shirt, he struck off in Baines's wake. The man, he reckoned, had been trying obliquely to warn him.

No lights were showing in the big house now. He wondered what thoughts were tramping through the girl's head. Was she pleased with the night's work or only more frightened, more cut off and desperate? She had taken a long chance.

He rasped his stubbled jaw, unconsciously bitter. The peace he had been looking for, the anodyne of anonymity, seemed as far from his reach as the westering moon. He felt old and defeated, as wrung out and frustrated as that poor wretch in the poem who'd been yoked to the albatross.

He sent a final wavering look about the yard. The shadows bulked longer, more opaque, as though a wagonload of ink had been dumped into the blue of them. A vagrant breeze cut through the cottonwoods, and somewhere, faint in the distance, a bunch of coyotes yammered, accentuating his isolation, pointing up the futilities of his life and bringing more blackly into his awareness that foreboding whose sharp teeth were seldom more than one jump behind.

Howlett's hand brushed the worn-smooth

butt of his pistol, making certain that if he should need it the heavy-calibered Colt would not hang in its leathers. He tugged the rim of his hat past his eyes and saw the bunkhouse light fade out. The groan of bunk ropes came through a window, and the reek of coal oil cut across the odors of dust and whisky and the effluvia from unwashed bodies.

He considered returning to the barn with his blankets, finally pushing the thought away, knowing he couldn't afford to. He walked on, finding the door still open, and stepped through, seeking a wall with the blades of his shoulders. The place couldn't have been much blacker if it had been stacked with stovelids. He had no idea which bunks were filled. Not all of these jaspers were asleep, yet none spoke.

He got a stinker from his hatband and left-handedly whipped it alight on his leg. Tendrils of flame sprang out of his cupped fingers, guiding his searching stare through the shadows. Only four bunks were occupied; it took him a little longer to make sure Baines wasn't here. Someone sleepily swore and turned over. A horse-faced individual snarled, "Chris' sakes, feller!"

Howlett let the match die, more disturbed than he could find reason for. He stood against the wall, darkly thinking. There were six in the crew, not counting the foreman. One was pounding his butt toward the county seat. Four were in here. Where the hell had Baines got to? He dropped his blankets onto a bunk, started to pull off his boots, then very quietly straightened. He went back outside.

The night appeared noticeably cooler. Or was this nerves?

He'd lost track of Baines coming over from the barn, but the man had certainly been headed in this direction. There were no buildings beyond the bunkhouse. Back the other way were the smithy, a wagon shed, a one-room shack that was probably Virgen's headquarters, and the barn. The house was across the yard; Howlett would have noticed if Baines had cut over there. The fellow must have made his move between Virgen's shack and the smithy.

What had Baines seen or heard to pull him over there? Why hadn't he come back? He might have gone for a horse, but he couldn't have got away on one without someone hearing.

Howlett's long-fingered hand touched the wood of his gun again. He was remembering the huddle of men standing around, the blaze of lamps which had greeted his arrival with Frances Tappen. Had these been connected with the girl's protracted absence or with something which had not yet been disclosed? He recalled what she had told him about this outfit's reputation, about the series of unreasonable happenings which had reduced the crew by approximately half. A cold wind blew across the back of his neck.

Those fellows just hadn't casually managed to get hurt. He recalled the ugly laugh with which Bill Virgen had walked away.

He faded into the gloom of the cottonwoods, hugging the spots that were blackest. Had Baines been trying to be friendly or trying to lead the new man into a box? With frequent stops, Howlett presently hauled up behind the back of the smithy. Old boards softly rattled in the grip of the breeze. He caught the settling of timbers but no sound of human activity.

He drifted around the wall that was nearest, the denser blotch of the bunkhouse vaguely glimpsed off there to the right, and stood listening a moment to the bump of his heart. He was taking a god-awful chance prowling this way. Virgen, if they ran into each other, wouldn't waste any time with talk.

Howlett, scarcely breathing, moved on.

The shop's door was held open with balingwire. Howlett, eyeing that black rectangle, felt sweat spring through the pores of his skin. The rank breath of danger was all around him, but he had to know. He lifted the gun from his hip and went in fast.

For long seconds nothing happened; after further listening, he struck another match, snuffing the flame of it almost at once. The place was empty.

He came back to the doorway and grimly stood studying the night. Though he could not see them because they were set back, the corrals were between this shop and the wagon shed, with the wind coming through them, lazily whirling the blades of the mill which fed the troughs.

The horses were quiet. And this was odd' for even though they could not see him or catch his scent they oughtn't to be completely motionless. There was a wildness threading this roundabout blackness, a feeling of danger that lifted Howlett's hackles.

He bent and cautiously felt about for something he could pick up and throw. It wasn't the oldness of the dodge which made him finally decide against it. Call it hunch if you want. A man who put his trust in a gun, however unwillingly, learned the truth about hunches.

He straightened and moved out into the night, once again stopping to listen. Not even a hoof stamp!

The moon was gone; nothing was left but starlight and the sense of time running out and a heightened foreboding. He moved again a few steps with all his sharpened instincts protesting, desperately urging him to give this up. Danger was all about him now, hemming him in with its electrified tension, so near he thought he could almost smell it.

He stood within a stride of the shop's corner, the one nearest Virgen's quarters, which he could not see but which, to the best of his remembrance, were perhaps seventy feet away. The corrals, once he pushed out of his tracks, would be half that distance to the left of him. He couldn't see anything that resembed a man. The cottonwoods, mostly, were around the corrals, but the pooled gloom trapped by their heavy foliage reduced visibility practically to zero. Had someone been crouching three feet away Howlett was sure they would not have seen each other. The danger he could almost smell would be around the corner, listening just as he was, waiting, gun lifted, for the move or sound that must inevitably come.

Only a fool would stand still while death stalked him. He was on Star Cross where things didn't just happen but were engineered with considerable care, hand-tailored and directed by a malign intelligence that would balk at nothing to get what it wanted. *It's a rough country,* Rimrose had told him, but he had come anyway. And now they were out to get rid of him. Whoever was after him could afford to wait out the whole goddam night!

Howlett moved toward the yard with one wide-springing stride that set him down on yielding flesh that twisted and gave and dropped him sprawling. Like the pounce of a panther something came at him as, desperately, he tried to gather himself, to find his lost pistol, to get his legs under him. He was frantic. And then he was nothing, everything dissolving in one great burst of light.

SEVEN

TALK finally roused him, the incessant pulsations of uncountable words whirling over and around him like sound in a seashell, now climbing, now falling, meaningless but constant until the nagging recurrence of continually repeated cadences irascibly prodded his mind back toward reality. Feeling came then, gigantic charges of pain that roared through his head like surf across a shingle. Somewhere, beyond this, there were indefinable pressures and a terrible sense of strangling. "Pick him up," a voice said gruffly; and Howlett, alarmed, jerked open his eyes.

Panic hit him. Nothing was clear. He seemed to be staring into a kind of vermilion mush mixed with darkness and tendrilly tufts and pale fragments of something that looked like bone. Both his arms were grasped, and each of his legs at the knee. The red mush dropped away as he was lifted. He was staring, face downward, at the back of a man's horribly mangled head. The ground swayed above a forest of blurred legs that queerly had no bodies and were tramping upside down.

"Let him go!"

He hardly recognized Frankie's voice.

All movement stopped. Though distracted by pain and dizziness, Howlett tried to lift his head. But try as he would, he could not do it—not with them carrying him belly down.

Virgen said, "Now, God damn it—"

"Down!" Frankie cried. Plainly, it wouldn't take much to send her into hysteria.

The men let go. The ground slapped most of the air out of Howlett. When he got back enough sense to know what he was doing, he got an arm under him and struggled onto his knees. It took a bit longer to get the rest of the way up but he finally made it, staggering around as if on stilts. When the ground quit pitching and his eyes came into focus, he knew how near he'd been to reaching the end of the line.

Every lamp on the place must have been lighted, and half the lanterns. The crew was standing around with their eyes like the muzzles of twin-barreled Greeners. The only thing holding them back was Frankie's gun. Thinly she said, "Get over here, Howlett."

Behind the bristle of his mustache Virgen's mouth tightened ominously. "That ain't goin' to help him. Ain't goin' to help you none, neither. We caught this sorry son red-handed—lookit the blood on him! Lookit his gun!"

"There'd be blood on anyone sprawled like that across Baines."

"He was that way 'fore I ever put hand to him. I heard this here groanin'. I come bustin' over.

There the guy was, a-straddlin' Baines and beatin' his brains out! If you ain't goin' to stand up for your boys—"

"You've been over all that but you still haven't said why."

"Why! Virgen's glance swirled around. He said with a blustery impatience, "How would *I* know? This saddle tramp—"

"And all that groaning," Frankie said. "I don't think Baines had any time to groan."

"Never said it was Baines. All I know is I heard it. I come running, and here this bum was beatin' the hell out of him with that pistol." The foreman looked at her maliciously. "Them's facts you ain't goin' to be able to get around." He showed a cold-jawed amusement. "May God strike me dead if that ain't every word the truth!"

The flutelike notes of a bird's call climbed through the sudden quiet.

"I expect God's busy right now," she said dryly. "I find it hard to believe one man would kill another so brutally over nothing. Howlett had just arrived; he'd never seen Baines before—"

"We don't know that. They had words in the barn. Like I told you, this feller Howlett was plumb wound up! He was tryin' to auger Baines into some kind of deal. Baines walked away. Howlett must've gone after him. . . .Anyhow, what matters is he done it!"

"We've got only your word for that"

"You callin' me a liar?"

"I'm pointing out a fact."

Howlett's throbbing head felt as big as a washtub, but he was taking this in. Of the men standing around, only the foreman was fully dressed. Frances had a blue wrapper clutched round her. The green eyes looked too big for her face, but the barrel of her pistol never wavered from Virgen's chest. The foreman, although seeming to give little attention to it, knew what could happen if the thing went off.

His tongue crept out and crossed dry lips. "Send him in to the law then. I'll make out a writin'."

Howlett looked at all of them. The fury was out of him, and despite his throbbing head he could see plainly that the crew was impressed. Virgen's talk made sense to them. One still appeared somewhat dubious, but the rest took Virgen's word for gospel. The girl had found flaws, but even here the big foreman had bested her, letting words from her own mouth estrange her from the crew.

Howlett's shoulders moved. "Suits me," he said, and saw the satisfaction that swept through the foreman's eyes.

But the girl saw it too. In a pinch she could show a lot of coolness herself. Howlett's opinion of her intelligence rose considerably when she elected to let this ride for the moment. "I'll have grub—"

"These boys," Virgen said, "have a right to know how you stand on this. You're sendin' him in?"

She said flatly, "No."

"You're goin' to see this grifter get away with it? After me catchin' him red-handed? How do you figure these boys'll feel havin' a sidewinder sharin' their blankets that just got done murderin' one of their buddies?"

Indignation was bright in the green of Frankie's stare. "They're not going to like it by the time you get through with them, but I'm still the final word around here and as long as I'm footing the bills I'll have it!" She stood there a moment, breathing hard, cheeks flushed. Howlett saw Virgen's eyes widen a little, but the man let it pass. She went on. "I'll have grub on the table in about fifteen minutes. After we've eaten," turning to Howlett, "you catch up your horse and start looking for strays."

"I'll want that belt gun."

"Give it to him," Frances said.

"Wait a minute." Virgen scowled. He shot a quick look around. "That pistol's evidence—"

"I'll be responsible."

"You're pilin' up a heap of grief—"

"You can ride in and talk to the sheriff about it. Just give him the gun. After all that talk, he's likely to need it."

Narrowing lids shut away Virgen's thoughts. For perhaps three seconds he stood without moving. Finally he brought the weapon from one of his hip pockets, stripped the neckerchief off the blood-discolored barrel and tossed the gun to Howlett. "Right now I wouldn't give a dollar for this spread."

"Right now," Howlett said in a quiet, toneless way, "you'd better start keeping some of those thoughts to yourself."

EIGHT

APPARENTLY Frances Tappen cooked for the whole outfit.

The eastern sky was beginning to pale with false dawn when, ten minutes later, having shaved and washed and put on his other shirt, Howlett tramped over to the west wing of the big house and presented himself at the kitchen screen. In the light of two bracket lamps he could see the scrubbed table and, against one wall, shelves laden with crockery. Coffee bubbled in a chipped agateware pot. A platter of hot biscuits on the table caught his eye, and the smell of frying ham and eggs made him realize he was astonishingly hungry. The girl looked up from the stove. "Come on in." She waved a hand toward a box on a bench by the sink. "Eating irons —grab a plate and fly at it."

He got a plate, a cup that was big as a barber's mug, and a fork and knife. As she filled his cup with java black and stout, her eyes came up, deeply shadowed, and worried when he did not at once reach forward his plate. A small and desperate smile crossed her mouth. "It won't be easy."

"It's not that," he said, and stopped, half ashamed, filled with confusion and stubbornness and anger. How could he make her see how he felt? How explain the despair nearly turning him crazy at the prospect of what he saw shaping so clearly? He had to get away! Yet how could a woman understand a thing like that?

He was still without movement, still groping for words when the screen door was shoved back; the crew filed in, solemnly shucking their hats and appearing about as happy as a gather of tenderfoot trappers convened to get the hide off a skunk.

Intuition warned her. She leaned forward to peer up into his face, looking frightened and lost, indescribably forsaken. Virgen stood idle against the doorframe, watching. The girl gave a nervous laugh. "You want this grub or don't you?"

Howlett held out his plate, cursing under his breath as the line formed behind him, boots scraping up sound into the thickening quiet. There was no joshing or horseplay. He took his plate to the table, gooseflesh roughening the arms beneath his shirtsleeves, and pulled out a chair near the end of the table where there'd be nothing behind him but solid wall. One by one the others followed, settling their elbows along the scrubbed planks, Virgen taking the chair at the head. There still wasn't any talk, a fact normal enough around most outfits but here so darkly suggestive it set Howlett's teeth on edge.

Eating, he watched Frankie, covertly studying her.

Virgen pushed back, reaching into his vest for the makings, while the girl came around with more coffee. With his brownpaper quirly rolled and fired, the foreman stared, darkly thoughtful. "Goin' to be uncommon hard," he said, "tryin' to keep work up with riffraff prowlin' through these hills and havin' always to keep one eye out behind you." He looked around at her then. "Still," he said, "I expect we'll make out to do what we have to do." and let the silence drift in while his eyes flattened out with a kind of amusement. "This here new feller, now, likely won't be inhabitin' these parts no great while."

Howlett's face didn't change but he could feel the dark anger coming alive in him deep down. A sick feeling began gnawing him, and half-forgotten faces rose out of his past, strengthening him in his faltering intention, reminding him that, however it looked, flight was indeed his only "out" from this trap. To stay would only pile up more dead without in any way materially benefiting Frankie. Star Cross was lost—common sense told him that. He could feel her gaze, all the hopes and fears that were in her crying out to him. But he kept his mouth shut, staring doggedly at the mopped-up surface of his plate.

Virgen laughed.

The agateware pot struck sharp against the stove, a sound that was filled with rebellion. Suddenly she cried almost hysterically: "He'll be here as long as any of you! Star Cross belongs to him—*do you figure he's going to let you run him away from it?"*

Howlett's eyes were live coals as he kicked free of the chair, flinging onto his feet with a spread-fingered hand crouched over the butt of his gun. He was not his own master. She had cut the ground from under him.

The girl's eyes shone with a sharp, sudden joy. The crew, drop-jawed, sat rigid, hypnotically dominated by Howlett's look. No word was spoken, or necessary. The thing they saw straining back of that stare held them frozen.

Excitement pushed the girl into speech, her words tumbling over each other. "You'll find out! Some of you must have been wondering about Lippy—he's bound for the county seat with a quitclaim! This ranch will stand in the name of White Howlett. You'll take your orders hereafter from him!"

One of the hands—a squarehead down in the books as Flat Top—pushed away from the table and got off his butt. "Not me," he growled. "I've had enough!" The drag of his spurs clinked over the floor, eyes touching no one's till he gripped the screen's latch. With his head swiveled around he said over a shoulder, looking riled at the girl, "I'd of stuck till hell froze, but I ain't holdin' out fer what Baines got—not, by God, fer no saddle-tramp foreigner!"

"If you expect to get paid . . ." This was Virgen again.

The puncher went out, the door slamming behind him.

Two men, Howlett saw, had their eyes skinned at Virgen. Now one of these got up. "Them's my sentiments right down to the ground!" The screen slapped again. Virgen shrugged. That man, Howlett guessed, would make straight to Rimrose by the shortest cut.

He had to admire Virgen's slickness; he hadn't seen the man cued; he hadn't glimpsed one thing beyond that watchful attention. But the watchers, he was sure now, were Virgen's pair of imports—not the first one, he hadn't the look of it. It was plain as plowed ground, if one needed further evidence, that Baines had been one of the old Star Cross crew, the four who had stuck, Flat Top too, and the one who was fanning the breeze with that quitclaim. The fourth man, still here, would be the big-bellied one with the mole on his chin. "What's your monicker?" Howlett said.

"Beauty."

"You hauling freight too?"

"I'll look at your hole card."

"How about you?" Howlett said to Virgen's hardcase.

"Reckon I'll hang an' rattle a while."

"I'll stick," Virgen said, "if you ain't got no one in mind for this job."

Howlett weighed the man with an irascible glance, not fooled for a second by this easy assurance but knowing, as did Virgen, no ranch could be worked in this country without riders. A case of damned if he did and damned if he didn't. He was still convinced there'd be no holding this spread, but if he could market the beef he might save the girl something. It struck him then that he might just as well go whole hog while he was at it. "Do the work," he said, "and the job's still yours. We'll ride as soon as the chuck wagon's loaded."

Virgen said blandly, "You're goin' to try for a roundup?"

"I'm scraping this range clean."

A haze of exhaled tobacco smoke splayed around Virgen's face. "No need to wait on the wagon," he said. "Miz' Frankie'll catch up." He stubbed out his cigarette. "She knows this range well as I do. We'll start at South Pass—"

"We'll start"—Howlett smiled—"at the north end of Star Cross, pushing everything ahead of us, cleaning it out as we go. And we'll all go together." He reckoned anything Virgen wanted would be better done exactly opposite.

Virgen eyed him intently. "You figure on takin' this drive through to Naco?"

Howlett listened to the sound of departing hoofs. He told Beauty, "Get your plunder gathered up and go fetch in the cavvy." To Virgen's man he said: "Bring up the wagon and get a team ready. When you've got that taken care of, you can load in whatever supplies we're like to need, and do anything else Miss Frankie wants tended."

The man jerked a nod and followed Beauty out. Howlett looked at Virgen. "You'll know all about that when the time comes. While you're standing around, you can break out a shovel and get Baines planted."

The burly foreman stared, his eyes like buffed agate, then scooped up his hat without a word and stomped off. Howlett stood a moment thinking, not liking any part of this. He sloshed on his own hat, knowing that nothing was really holding him except this girl's smartness. Without pride he could go. She had seen that, deliberately banked on it, knowing that without pride a gunfighter was nothing. *White* Howlett, she'd said. He didn't like that either. He went through the screen without looking back at her.

Howlett was not fooled by Virgen's complacence. The foreman, hating him, would have left in a minute if his presence someplace else could have served Rimrose better. Howlett, knowing he was coddling a viper, could see no way out: they were so shorthanded they were going to have to put up with the man. He could hear the rasp and scrape of Virgen's shovel and, from the barn, the half-caught sound of Virgen's hardcase swearing as he yanked and cuffed at the team he was readying.

The pressure of time, with its ever increasing possibility of recognition and the continual danger of direct action stemming out of Rimrose's wrath, posed a burden which Howlett found well-nigh intolerable. Nor could he doubt the sharpness of the girl's judgment now; he could only wonder on the wheel of what grim experience it had been ground. So much about her was wholly baffling and contradictory. He was outraged by the way she had used him, yet drawn by something deep and richly emotional buried deep within her. He tried to convince himself that what he sensed could not be there, that her barren silences were exactly that, and cloaked no mysteries—hid nothing but emptiness; that what she stirred was no more than the hungers of any man kept too long away from women. But he could not get her out of his head. He was alternately self-condemning and raging bitter against her, but she had handled him right. He was stuck now, held not by her need but by the pride she had uncovered. He cursed himself for a fool and cut over toward the smithy for another look at Baines.

Wind roved the yard, bringing the smells of dust and death, and even more noticeably the feeling of futility which seemed to permeate everything at Star Cross.

Howlett found the body by stumbling into it again. He bent down, slipping the puncher's gun from leather, and crouched there silently holding it for a moment. It was his fate, he reckoned, to be fruitlessly searching for answers that eluded him. Whether he was right about the girl or not, he had no intention of exploring the possibilities. No man in his position, no man with his kind of background, had any business even considering such thoughts.

He slipped Baines's gun into his left boot and got up, disturbed and shaken. He knew himself too well from the past to have any faith at all in his future. The future was what you shared with a woman. . . . He cursed again, wheeling sharply, and cut over to the barn, stepping back as Virgen's man came out with the harnessed team.

"What are you called?" Howlett said.

"Name's Kidder." The man gave him a hard look and went on.

Howlett listened to the wind, wondering how long it would take Beauty to fetch in the horses. He hunched his shoulders, comparing what must be done and the men he had to work with, and finding no reasonable balance. Rimrose would never let this drive alone. *Rough country out there* . . .

He went into the barn and put his gear on the buckskin, leading him out. Near the trough he paused, surprised not to catch any sound of Virgen's shovel. The earth had a luminous shine to it now; mountains to the east were showing their ragged crests as a sharper black against the sky. As his circling glance took in the house, he froze. The reins dropped, forgotten. Cold rage swelled in his throat as lamp-thrown shadows reeled across a drawn shade. He raced across the yard and slammed the screen back with a violence that nearly tore it from the hinges.

Inside the room one shuddery breath made a whisper of sound.

No one moved.

Howlett said, "I guess, Virgen, you don't hear very good."

NINE

BROKEN crockery from the collapsed shelf was shining underfoot. Virgen had Frankie backed against the ledge of the table, with one arm caught behind her. He was savagely striving to throw her down. His hat was gone, and the girl's free hand was desperately clenched in the slack of his shirt. He was like a bull, but she was frantic. Her hair was loose, and the gleaming round of one bare shoulder shone whitely through the rip of her dress. Her eyes were enormous, and she was sobbing. Her shaking legs buckled under her when the foreman let go.

Caution held Virgen locked in his tracks, swollen with hate, still half bent over her while a gust of wind rattled a blind on its roller. He wheeled, revealing flushed cheeks that were livid with scratches.

"I gave you a job," Howlett grated. "Why aren't you tending it?"

"She's been playin' her tricks on half the men in this crew!"

Howlett stared, silent, thumbs hooked in his shell belt. There was no expression on his face.

Only his eyes, blackly shining, showed the depth of his temper.

"Sure, it's *you* right now she's got her sights on—yesterday I was brass-collar dog!" Virgen, shifting weight, turned with great care, but he could not keep all his spleen tied up. "Tomorrow—"

"We'll take care of when it gets here," Howlett said. "Today you dig. Right now. Get at it!"

Virgen's stare grew bright with outrage. He bent, snatching viciously at the butt of his gun.

With a cry of dismay Frankie gathered herself. Howlett said, "Keep out of this!" and walked up to Virgen, watching the man, not hurrying, not stopping until their chests were a hand's span apart. Howlett's eyes were steel. "Now. Drag your gun."

Virgen's stare grew desperate. Sweat crept out on his face, but his gun stayed where it was. So did Virgen. What he saw was death! The lust to kill was in Howlett's eyes. Virgen had killed—more than once—but he knew in his bones who would go if he touched iron.

A shudder ran over him. He tried to moisten his lips.

Howlett's smile was a grimace. "You'd better get started."

Virgen's knees were weak and his whole body trembled. His eyes slid away. "Yeah," he said huskily. "This drive's the important thing . . ."

That notion, doggedly clung to, held Virgen

up until he got to the door. There shame over-
took him, and his uncertainty, dread, caution—
even the allegiance he owed Harry Rimrose—all
were scattered like straws in the wind. He cried
in a high, half-strangled voice: "She's nothin' t'
me—understand? Not a thing! If she was I'd by
God kill you, mister!" The emerald flashed on
his littlest finger as he slammed open the screen.

Howlett let him go, and wanted nothing so
much as to be done with all of it. He moved his
head tiredly, feeling older than Noah, and found
the girl staring unseeingly into space. She felt his
look. Her eyes met his and turned away. Seldom
had Howlett seen anything more blankly hope-
less than the way her hands fluttered up and then
fell.

Howlett walked over to where she still pressed
against the table. She moved away from it a little, one hand coming up to hold her torn dress
together. He put a hand on her shoulder, intend-
ing encouragement, and felt the warm flesh
shrink from his touch. He took his hand away
quickly.

The silence became even more unendurable.

A rumor of hoofs crept out of the wind. Self-
conscious, Howlett said, "This drive . . . At least
it will bring things into the open. We may be
able to salvage something for you." The hoofbeats were plain now. Howlett, listening,
growled, "One horse," and his forehead
tightened into an uneasy frown. "If that's Beauty—"

"Not Beauty," she sighed, looking up at him

then. "Those hoofbeats are coming from the direction of town."

She followed him into the yard. Virgen's man, Kidder, drove up with the wagon, stopping the team just past the screen door. He'd heard too, and had his head canted, listening. Frankie's eyes went back to Howlett. In the early light she saw the grim set of his shoulders, the depth of the lines graven round his mouth.

Howlett said, "Get a pencil and paper and I'll quitclaim it back to you."

She looked away from him then, all twisted inside. In a small voice she said, putting a hand out to touch him, "I'm sorry ..."

"You didn't like that back there. In spite of the mauling." He jerked a nod toward the house. "If you can't stand the thought of a killing why'd you saddle me with your troubles? You knew what I'd do—you saw deeper into me than I ever have myself." He swung away from her. "A man's got to follow his bent, I reckon."

Her fingers convulsively tightened on his arm. "You're not that way—not really, deep down."

"Stop fooling yourself."

"You're not!" Something clean and fresh, immeasurably stirring, came from her to him. Her whole look seemed to change, transfigured with an inner beauty.

"You're bitter and angry and cynical now, but you're not that way. You're kind and good—"

"You fool!" Howlett whispered. His eyes blazed at her. "Don't read into me ..." He stopped, jaws clenched, as though struck by a bullet. His whole face turned queer. He laughed at her then, filling the sound with a scorn and contempt that drove her, white of cheek, back. "You wanted a gun—you've got one. Don't try to pull anything else out of the hat."

He saw Kidder comfortably perched on the wagon, his sly little eyes taking all of this in. The girl saw Kidder grin.

A pistol jumped into Howlett's fist, muzzle lifting. Kidder's jaw dropped a foot. "Gawd's sakes!" the man yelled. "I ain't done nothin'!"

"Climb down and start loading that wagon."

Kidder almost fell off.

Howlett, pouching his gun, strode after his horse. The buckskin whickered. Horses spilled from the cottonwoods. Howlett saw Beauty then swinging handily around them, shunting them into the bullpen beyond.

His mind was still full of Frankie when he was brought up short, stricken helpless, by the stunning and completely unexpected impact of a shotgun's muzzle driven into his back.

"Steady does it! Move one finger and I'll blow you to Halifax!"

TEN

THERE was a coldly bristling satisfaction in the burr of that rasping voice that even through the girl's muffled scream warned Howlett.

"Now unshackle that hogleg."

The belt, sliding away from Howlett's waist, thumped the ground.

"Don't see where they got the idee you was tough. All right, Kidder—git that rifle."

When Virgen's man, grinning, backed off with the saddle gun, the fellow who was calling the turns said, "You kin come around now and point that *bayo coyote* toward town. If I have any trouble, there's gonna be *three* stiffs fer Coroner to set on."

It was Vaguely's day man, Anvil Orso, Howlett discovered when he got squared around. He saw Frankie. "Watch her, Orso!" Kidder growled. In the brightening light Howlett saw the girl stooping to pick up his dropped cartridge belt.

Orso's spidery eyes watched the lot of them.

Virgen, bland as butter, sauntered out of the trees with an easy smile. The girl looked indignant as, straightening, she fed the strap end of the belt into its buckle and draped the heavy harness over the torn shoulder of her dress.

Howlett, somberly studying the jailer where he now stood in the stirrups of a mouse-colored livery mare, knew it wouldn't take much to turn the yard into a shambles. Orso would shoot at the drop of a hat.

"He owns Star Cross now," Frankie cried. "You can't—"

Orso grinned. "Git goin'," he said to Howlett.

The inquest on Cretch and Crispen was held in the Bucket of Suds saloon. All the chairs and tables had been stacked in a corner. Space had been roped off before the bar for the coroner, the two bodies, Vaguely, Howlett and Orso, who was still packing his double-barreled Greener. Butterball Benson, a tub of a man with quivering chins and a cupid's-bow mouth he seemed incapable of closing, was the officiating officer. He'd been boosted with considerable horseplay to a perch on the top of the bar. Someone had fetched him a bottle of whisky, and he hulked there beside it, mouth working like a fish out of water, multiple chins jiggling to each wheeze of his breath.

Howlett, seated between Undersheriff Jim Vaguely and the shotgun-fondling Orso, saw Rimrose standing in a group of hard-faced riders at the front of the crowd, sardonically eyeing the uncomfortably self-conscious jurymen the coroner had impaneled and segregated just beyond the rope and close by the door to the big-stakes poker room.

Howlett had arrived in Blind Mule with Orso some fifteen minutes earlier; the bulk of this interval had been spent bringing Vaguely up to date with events at Star Cross. The deputy's nods had looked both worried and nervous. He had chewed the inside of his cheek without comment, sending Howlett ahead of him with Orso. They had had their work cut out getting in. The place bulged at the seams with grousing out-of-work miners, most of whom appeared to have convicted Howlett already.

"Hear ye! Hear ye!" Orso intoned.

Butterball Benson badgered the cork from his bottle, downed about a tumblerful, gulped for breath and beat on the bar with a bungstarter. "This court'll come to order!"

He smeared the back of a sleeve across the moist shine of his chins and sent a glare at the fussed jurymen. "We're here to make out if these deaths is the result of murder, suicide or accident. In bringing in a verdict it'll be up to you wallopers to determine whether further investigation is called for." He paused for another clutch at the bottle, every eye in the place but the two pairs on the floor watching his throat move around its gurgle, and more than several of this conclave licking their lips in envy.

"Now," Butterball said, perking up a little, "in this kinda weather time is of the essence. Sheriff, can you identify these bodies?"

Jim Vaguely got up. "Feller on the left is Cretch, like you know. Other one's Crispen. Between them they owned—"

"We know about that. What we don't know is how a pair of important moguls like them come to be here in this kinda shape."

"Well," Vaguely said, "I had 'em stashed in the icehouse—"

Butterball, glowering, beat on the bar. "Sheriff wasn't figuring to be funny! Now then, Jim, please relate in your own words how you come to be in possession of these here bodies."

"Well, sir, quite a piece after dark on the night of the twenty-third a feller dressed like a cowpuncher packed them into the alley between this place and my office."

"Packed them how?"

"He had 'em lashed onto the backs of their horses."

"You recognized this feller?"

"I hadn't never saw him before."

"But you recognized the bodies?"

"Ain't a man in this town wouldn't of known Cretch an' Crispen. They been losin a lot of payrolls to road agents operatin' around these parts. This month they figured to try gettin' it through theirselves."

"You was nacherly surprised when you—"

"Not too surprised, no. I didn't reckon they'd do any better than the stages. Fact is, I'd done my best to talk em out of it. When they wouldn't hear to that I offered to send my deputies with 'em—"

"You mean by 'deputies' your jailers Orso and Hanley?"

"They're deputies, ain't they? They been swore in—"

Butterball thumped his bungstarter again. "That's enough of that racket! Now, Jim, what about this feller that brought in the bodies: you'd know him again if you seen him?"

"There he sits, right there. Name's Howlett."

"What did he have to say for himself?" Butterball asked, ignoring the black looks.

"I expect we'd better let him tell that himself," Vaguely said, beckoning Howlett.

Howlett stood up, ignoring the hard looks focused on him by the crowd. In simple words, and without embroidery, he told of hearing the shots, of coming onto the scene of the shooting and the resultant conversation which had caused him to come into Blind Mule with the bodies. There was an indignant racket from the mining portion of the audience when he related the counterfeiting angle and described the saddlebags crammed with "fake" banknotes.

Butterball beat on the bar again. He said, when some semblance of order was restored, "Being a stranger, I guess you couldn't know any different." He wiped off his face with a purple bandanna and had brief recourse to the bottle, smacking his lips. Then he wheezed a while in silence, seeming to be scanning something inside his head. "Would you know that feller if you seen him again?"

"I reckon I would," Howlett said, and the

room got so quiet the droning of flies assumed almost the proportions of an orchestral accompaniment.

"Could you describe him?"

"I think so."

"Well," said Butterball testily, "get at it!"

"One of the things," Howlett said, "which impressed me the most about this fellow was a kind of driving energy that seemed to come out of him even when he was still. He had bold, lively features—"

"Wait a minute," Butterball said. "I'm not quite sure I get that picture. About this 'driving energy'—can't you put that plainer?"

"It was a kind of aggressive impatience, an intolerance of obstacles—of delay or frustration of any sort. A kind of arrogance, as though he knew all the answers and looked on anyone who didn't as downright stupid—practically ready for a string of spools."

"All right." Butterball nodded. "I guess we've got that straight. He'd let on to you he was a Federal marshal, one of them man-huntin' sonsabitches that would foller a feller's trail till hell froze and then skate back with him over the ice. What about his hair, face, general build?"

"Pretty solid put together. Chesty, thick neck —kind you find on a studhorse that's run out all year with a brand of mares. Weight about . . ." Howlett, pausing, deliberately turned, looking square at Rimrose, saying into the startled silence, "about two-ten. Cornsilk hair. Roman nose. Skull in back goes straight up from the collar."

There was a chorus of gasps.

Harry Rimrose laughed. "Man, you're wasting your breath. When those two fellers was being gulched, I was the largest part of twenty miles away. Out at my Number Four camp, as it happens, readin' sign on rustlers."

Butterball said, "You can prove that, I guess?"

"There was eight fellers with me—"

"Some of them hardrocks you got around you now?"

With his lips pulled back from his teeth, Rimrose said, "Some of my crew, yes."

"I don't know," Butterball said, looking down his nose, "whether them kinda rannies constitutes proof or not. Likely they'd say whatever you told 'em."

The rancher's eyes slimmed down, a cold rage sparkling through the slots of his stare. While he was squirming to get on top of his anger one of the jurymen, a round-faced fellow in an elegant brown derby and a chin-choker shirt with a green scarf fastened biblike across it, pushing forward against the rope, called out: "What time was it, stranger, when you come into that clearin'?"

Howlett, considering those shrewd eyes above the juryman's apple-round cheeks, remembered the man as the derby-hatted gent who'd sung out, "Who you got there, pardner?" as he'd been riding into Blind Mule with these bodies—*Had it only been two days ago?*

"I expect," he said, "it—"

"Hold on, Howlett!" Butterball shouted. "That better wait till we hear what time Two Pole Pumpkin was out to that line camp unravelin' sign!"

"Why," said Rimrose calmly, "it couldn't of been much more than half an hour short of dark. Ain't that about right, boys?"

There were grunts and nods from the group around him, Vaguely and the coroner swapping grim glances. "All right, Howlett," Butterball growled, "you can answer O'Mansky's question now."

But the juryman, gimlet-eyed, was staring at Rimrose. Before Howlett could speak, O'Mansky said, sharp with suspicion, "How'd you know, Rimrose, to fit that time so slick to your need?"

"But I didn't." The rancher smiled. "It only helps when you stop to figure out the distance I'd of had to travel to get there. It just coudn't be done. Cretch and Crispen was killed before sundown."

"That's right." Howlett nodded.

O'Mansky, watching Rimrose like a cougar ready to spring said, soft as dropping feathers, "And how did you know *that!*"

ELEVEN

RIMROSE saw in an instant the trap he'd stepped into through a too complete knowledge of what had happened in the clearing. In shaping his alibi he'd thought of just about everything but the fact that the time of the shooting had not been made public. Something dry and deadly seemed to creep through the room as those sleepless eyes burned back at O'Mansky. Then Rimrose was laughing, waving a hand at the deputy who had come half out of his chair, and saying with the casual ruefulness of a man who has let a cat out of the bag, "I guess Jim must of told me when he came yesterday to see if I could recognize this hardcase Howlett."

The crowd was peering around with emotions about as confused as the look on Vaguely's face as that badly rattled lawman tried to remember if he could have been such a fool.

Rimrose didn't give him very much time. Looking over the crowd, disposed as always in a pinch to gamble long risks where there was chance for immediate benefit, he said with his ready arrogance: "Not that it makes any vast amount of difference. Fred Oaks was out there

—ask him. He can give you the where, when and why-for of whatever you want to know about my movements that evening."

Fred Oaks was owner of X Bar, a balingwire outfit which adjoined Two Pole Pumpkin along that end of its range that lay amongst a devil's own maze of box canyons and gulches. That Fred was also suspected, strictly outside his hearing, of knowing more than something about strayed cows which never turned up again rather tickled Rimrose's macabre sense of humor. "I guess," he said, on firm ground now, "Fred's word ought to be about as good as this drifter's."

"Oaks," O'Mansky said, peering around, "isn't here."

Rimrose shrugged. "I can't help that." He grinned like a cat with a jawful of goldfish. "Ain't nothing to hinder you from riding out there if you want to." His Roman face whipped around to spear a hard look at Vaguely. "I don't know what you're up to, mister, but it seems like to me the law's going pretty far afield when it turns loose the only real suspect in this business to try and work up a case against—"

The rest of it was lost in the growling yells of the miners who were convinced almost to a man that the one to hang was the stranger, Howlett.

Butterball shouted himself into a fine sweat, putting a whole new series of marks into the top of the bar with his bungstarter. When he got enough quiet to make himself heard, he had to reach for lubrication before he could get any sound out. "If there's any more of this racket," he said, gulping and spluttering, "I'm gonna have Orso clear this place with that shotgun! Tell these fools why you turned Howlett loose, Sheriff."

Vaguely, looking as though he were being dragged through a knothole, reluctantly let go of his chair and straightened. Some of the healthy tan seemed rather yellow about his mouth; you could almost see him brace himself against the stares of all those scalp-hunting miners. He was in a bad spot, politically and physically. He suddenly tightened his jaw and plunged in. "There's a number of reasons why I turned Howlett loose. In the first place I couldn't believe any stranger would come up to the law with a pair of corpses and the story he peddled without there was a heap of real truth buried back of it."

The miners were starting to growl, but Vaguely now had the bit in his teeth. "I locked him up. I went out there and had a look at the place. Whoever killed that pair was plenty sure of himself—too sure, maybe," he said, looking at Rimrose. "There was plenty of sign bearin' out Howlett's story; I backtracked him clear up onto the rim. Then I went back an' started follerin' that 'marshal.' For about three miles his sign was plain as plowed ground. It left the scene of the shootin' on the same line of tracks he'd pointed out to Howlett as bein' the sign put down by the etcher he made out to be goin' after.

There wasn't any etcher—both sets of them tracks was made by the same horse. The killer's. I follered 'em up through the timber, through Crosscut Canyon and off around Bald Mesa where they turned in the shale and talus of the big slide north of Banning's Butte an' swung sharp east into the Barrens where I lost 'em amongst all that broken-up rock. If there's any one thing I'm sure of, it's that Howlett never killed either one of them fellers!"

He sat down, flushed, resentful, in a room gone quiet as hell on holiday. Butterball Benson picked up from there before any clamor from the crowd could tear loose. "The only other facts you need to know," he instructed the jury, "is that both Cretch and Crispen kicked off as a result of lead poisoning." He drifted a probing glance across their faces, staring appreciably longest at the derby-hatted O'Mansky. "If you feel—"

"Please the Court," O'Mansky said, "I've got another question."

"Well?"

"Was the same caliber bullet responsible for both deaths?"

Butterball nodded. It seemed that both Cretch and Crispen were struck from the front by .44/40's, though whether these were fired from a Winchester or one or more of Colt's Peacemaker pistols the coroner was not prepared to say.

"What was this stranger packin'?"

Butterball passed it to Vaguely. The sheriff's

deputy grudgingly admitted Howlett's saddle gun was a .44 Winchester, Model 1873. "He had a Peacemaker Colt in his bedroll."

The miners stirred restively, several of the more belligerent swapping grim looks.

"What about Two Pole Pumpkin there?"

"That don't mean a thing," Rimrose said. "Interchangeable cartridges have made both weapons popular. Half the fellers in this country—"

"All right," O'Mansky said, "I'll take your word for that much."

Butterball, catching the glitter beating up through Rimrose's stare, said hastily to the jury, "If I ain't said so before, you're to render your verdict according to the evidence you've gathered here right now. If you figure Cretch and Crispen—"

"What happened to all that cash?" one of the other jurors suddenly asked—"all that dough they was bringin' in for the payroll?"

Butterball, grimacing, said: "I don't know any more about that than you do. Now listen, men. If you feel Cretch and Crispen shot themselves you're to bring in a verdict of suicide. If you don't, and they didn't trip over their own guns, you can't make it anything else but murder. You've all heard what's been said here. Go into that back room and make up your minds."

Everybody and his uncle started talking at once no sooner than the door had slammed shut behind them. Butterball's fish mouth was clamped to the neck of his bottle again; then it came to him, sudden-like, that all these galoots sounding off with their notions wasn't going to be good for the ears of the jury, and he said, thumping the top of the bar till he could be heard, "If there's any more jabber I'm gonna clear this room!"

Three or four of the miners went right on jawing. The coroner glared around at Vaguely. Vaguely gave Orso the office, and the gangling jailer with his Greener hustled the trouble-makers out. After that there was quiet. Or a reasonable amount of it.

All but two of the big-hatted group about Rimrose took themselves off a few minutes later. Jim Vaguely looked worried. Butterball went back to his bottle. Orso scowled at Howlett. Howlett wondered what was happening at Star Cross, remembering how Virgen had been too smart to rush a gun held by a woman, remembering too how the foreman had looked when the new owner had stepped into the kitchen to find him trying to get Frankie down. He thought of other things, also, none of which improved his mental state.

He looked at the sweat dripping down over Butterball's chins. To get away from thoughts of Frankie he tried to put himself in Rimrose's place, in Virgen's—even in Vaguely's, but there was too much turmoil and commotion inside him. Why had Rimrose sent those jaspers outside? To have them in a position to break him loose if the verdict went against him? To box someone else? To cut a lick for Star Cross and the roundup Virgen probably hadn't even started?

The back-room door came suddenly open. All the muttering stopped. The jury came out with O'Mansky in the lead packing his derby carefully under an arm. They took up their places just beyond the roped-off bar.

"Well," Butterball said, looking them over, "have you brought in a true bill?"

O'Mansky fished a paper out of his bonnet, spent a crackly time getting the thing unfolded. "We, the gentlemen of this jury," he read, "mindful of our duty, do solemnly find the late lamented—"

"Never mind all that," wheezed Butterball testily. "Murder or suicide? Get to the meat of it."

"Murder by party or parties unknown."

Back at Star Cross, after Howlett had set off for town with the gangling Orso, Frances Tappen, stripped of hope, turned blindly into the ranch-house kitchen and, without even knowing she was doing it, barred the door. She had no confidence left—she hadn't anything. She'd put all her chips on the man she'd recruited from the Blind Mule jail, and now he was gone and she was alone, with no authority, completely at the mercy of whatever Bill Virgen was minded to do.

In her father's time there'd been no reason for

fear. She had done her best to hold the ranch together. She realized now that she should have fired Virgen the day her father died, and that Virgen—obviously allied with Rimrose—was behind everything that had happened to the ranch. She had tried to be the son her father had always wanted. Not only had she failed, but had even more miserably failed herself. She was twenty-six, with all the normal desires of a woman, but she had tried so long to fill a man's boots that now she couldn't even find the solace of tears. She was sick and tired of everything she knew. All she'd wanted to be was a woman, cherished and accorded a woman's rightful place. All she had found was the brute lust of Virgen. Desperate, she'd gambled everything on Howlett. Now he was gone, and she was alone and afraid.

The rope was torn loose in a stampede for the bar, each man augering at the top of his lungs. Rimrose and the pair he'd kept with him pushed out through the batwings in the wake of several miners hurrying streetward to spread the news. Orso, still clutching his Greener, looked disgusted. Nobody offered to help Butterball down.

Vaguely, catching hold of Howlett's arm, steered him through a back door into the jailyard alley. "Keep with me till you get armed," he growled.

But Howlett, pulling away from him, snarled, "I've got to get back to that ranch," and ran streetward.

His horse was gone from the hitchrack out front. He stopped short, breathing heavily, and spotted the glint of a rifle nosing out through the rails of a balcony across the way. Howlett, reaching downward, spun. Back of him Vaguely's gun crashed wickedly. The rifle dropped into the dust of the street, but two others opened up. Lead spatted into the planks all around. Something cuffed Howlett's shirt like a knife tearing through it. His hat jumped; then the deputy was shoving him stumbling ahead of him up the steps, yanking open the door and pushing him, swearing, into the office.

He slammed the door.

The derby-hatted juryman sat sprung back in the swivel with both feet cocked on the deputy's desk. "Little noisy out there. You suppose, Jim," he drawled, "there was anything to that yarn about Oaks?"

"Man's slipperier'n slobbers."

"Hadn't we better—" Howlett began, but the deputy said irritably:

"They tried and missed; they won't be out there now. One thing you've got to say for that feller: he don't waste no time runnin' around in circles. Irish, shake hands with this ranny. New boss out at Star Cross."

O'Mansky, reaching out, gave Howlett's fist a firm grip while Vaguely was getting the gun rack open. The deputy passed Howlett a rifle. The juryman gave him a narrowed, searching stare. "What happened to Willie Virgen?"

"Still foreman, I'm down as owner."

"Nice," O'Mansky said, "while it lasts. That won't be long if I know Virgen. You better get rid of him."

The deputy passed out a box of shells. Howlett began slipping brass into the Winchester. Vaguely gave him a six-shooter. O'Mansky said, "The things that can happen to a man out there . . ."

"We had a sample last night." Howlett told about Baines. Vaguely's jaws tightened.

"Proves my point," O'Mansky said. "You been uncommon lucky. He'll never rest now until—"

"I can't spare the man," Howlett said grimly. "She had only six, and two of those quit when I took over. Losing Baines leaves me just two hands I can halfway count on. I want to get those cows rounded up and sold while I've still got enough of them to give her a stake."

The dirty-hatted man nodded. Vaguely was hammering the planks of the back wall. When the door was cracked open he slipped through, shutting it after him. "Where you figuring to sell?" O'Mansky asked.

"Haven't had chance to—"

"Flagstaff's your best bet. They're cutting a heap of timber up there. Be a far piece to trail, but that lumber crowd'll pay good if you can make it. That's Mormon country all through them hills. They've got cows but they don't want that timber cut. You'll have trouble, all right, but at Naco or Tucson you won't clear two bucks a head. You might get as much as five from those lumberjacks."

Howlett's face was expressionless, but suddenly he knew he had to put aside his past and its ghosts. Looking behind would only make an old man of him. "Flagstaff's north?"

O'Mansky nodded. "Swing up through Winkelman, past Pinal Peak, skirtin' Globe on the west—"

"No market at Globe?"

"Damn' good market. Two Pole Pumpkin's got it sewed up, along with the reservation. If I was makin' that drive I'd take them up past Methodist Mountain, Rye, Payson, Pine. Near Clint's Well bear left. Stay right of Buck Mountain—that's just beyond Harris Park—and keep due north until you see a long narrow drink pointing northwest. That's Lake Mary. If you get that far you've got it made."

"Pretty long haul, is it?"

"About two hundred and fifty miles. You better not reckon on anything under a month—" He broke off in surprise as Vaguely, stepping into the office, was followed by Dollarosa and the night warden, Whiskers Hanley. Vaguely, crossing to the rack, broke out two more saddle guns. "There's the cartridges," he said, handing back three full boxes. Bending over the desk after dumping O'Mansky's feet, he dug out a pair of belt guns. "These fellers is goin' with you, Howlett. If you can't find nothin' else for em to do, put em to choppin' weeds."

Howlett wasn't quite sure he understood this deal. "If you're wanting to keep an eye on me—"

"They've got their reasons," Vaguely said, "and I've got mine. Be thankful those reasons come so handy to your need. Rimrose has upward of twenty men in his crew."

"And you're out to get him?"

Vaguely said flatly: "I can't do it alone. I don't think you can, either."

TWELVE

THEY pushed steadily through the late afternoon. Howlett's buckskin had been found, and both his companions were on good horses. There was very little talk. Each of them was keeping his eyes peeled sharp; there had been no sign of Rimrose's men when they left.

The gambler's presence wasn't bothering Howlett. He remembered Dollarosa telling him he'd grown up on a ranch and had lately been hankering to get back in a saddle. Either the fellow he had shot was on the road to recovery or Vaguely had made some kind of deal with him. But Whiskers was something else again.

Riding, Hanley looked a part of the horse. Howlett said presently, "You a native of these parts?"

Hanley showed a hard grin. "I can find my way around."

"I wasn't figuring to lose you," Howlett said dryly. "You repping for the law?"

Hanley's glance flashed over the backs of Howlett's hands. "You might call it that."

The jailer's attitude probably made sense. To

Howlett it was just one more irritation. They were making good time, though the buckskin was beginning to look pretty rocky when they finally pulled up to let them blow. Dollarosa, glancing around with a smile, said, "One will get you three nobody'll be home but the girl."

Howlett's face didn't change.

The gambler said: "Virgen's too slick not to carry out your orders. He'll figure bunching those cattle is just about the biggest favor a man could do Harry Rimrose."

Hanley, eyeing Howlett, said, "He'll take advantage of it."

Howlett shrugged. "He'll probably try."

"With twenty of the kind that hooligan hires you don't reckon anything we've got will stop him, do you?"

Howlett dourly put his horse into motion, not missing the speculative glint in Hanley's stare. When they were climbing the ridge that flanked Star Cross, Howlett said: "Whiskers, when a man has got his tail in a crack he's a heap apt to do most of his thinking from the muzzle of a six-shooter. Could be important to know who his friends are."

"That adds," Hanley grunted, even smiling a little in a cold sort of fashion that didn't much ease Howlett's mind.

"I would hate to find out, after I'd put a slug into him, that the guy I'd knocked over had been on my side of the fence."

Hanley's hard stare could have meant anything or nothing.

As they crested the ridge, Howlett saw the green swirl of hip-high grass, the Star Cross buildings, the chuck wagon and team still standing in the yard, the front feet of the horses fretfully stamping in the holes they had pawed. An unfamiliar tightness twisted something inside him and, almost as though he understood, Dollarosa, turning his head a little, murmured: "She's all right. The crew's gone, and Virgen with them. He'd never have left that team hitched."

With the gambler's concerned stare following him, Howlett, cruelly pushing the near foundered horse, dropped down off the bluff. Quickly, he was halfway across the waving green of the lush meadow. The two other men bunched forward over the horns of their saddles, each watching in the light of his own experience. Hanley abruptly said, "She'd have put the team up or used it."

"Not today. Put yourself in her place. Would she have pulled *any*one out of jail if she wasn't clear down to the bottom of the barrel? You heard Jim tell how things went over here. To count on him that way, deed the place to him, and then see him ride off with that trigger-loco Orso—Hell's fire, man, how would *you* feel in her boots! She's in a real bind; probably standing right now back of that door with a pistol."

They watched Howlett ride into the yard, quit the horse. Saw him crouch there a moment, head up, listening, then make for the house.

The warden's knuckles, over a fold of the

reins, showed white as scraped bone. "She's too good for that killer!"

"Don't you reckon he knows that?"

Hanley said bitterly, "Feller like that thinks of nothin' but himself." He lifted the reins, but the gambler's arm caught them.

"Man, can't you give them even these moments?"

Around Howlett shadows lay on the yard like the black crooked shapes of reaching fingers. Cursing, he ran toward the house. His shoulder struck the door in full fury. He felt the give of it as screws tore loose from the rotted casing, the thump of the falling bar plainly audible. Backing off, he drove at the barrier again. The top hinge went, and momentum tumbled him, off balance and sprawling, across the splintered panels.

It was all that saved him. Half blinded by the bursting flash of the gun, he heard the slap of the slug biting into the wall. He was up then, twisting, a gun in his own fist, hammer thumbed back, eyes colliding with the eyes of the girl above the shocked lift of the hand at her mouth. Staring, trembling, breathless, silent, trapped by emotions neither one could conceal, they were locked in their tracks for what seemed an eternity. Through smoke-clogged air the girl's appalled gaze burned with a terrible intensity in that interval as haunted, as anguished, as his own.

The gun fell out of her grip. She came to him, peering into his face. Her hands gripped his shoulders. The tips of her fingers traced the planes of his cheeks, moving lightly over the ridges of muscle, their touch a caress at the throb of his temples.

Howlett stood frozen. "Howlett—Howlett . . ." she said trembling.

He couldn't speak. All the reasons he had raised against this moment fell in clattering fragments. He took her, folding her to him with a groan of passion and despair.

The horses were in the yard, answering the team's called greetings, before the noise of their hoofs penetrated Howlett's mind, bringing him back to grim reality. The room was gray with encroaching night. It was dog eat dog—kill or be killed. He had come full circle. All his running and all of his thinking hadn't changed a thing.

He put Frankie away from him gently and, turning, found Hanley and the gambler watching from their saddles outside the broken door. The gambler's face was a crumpled mask. Behind his whiskers Hanley's expression was unreadable, but his eyes glittered.

Howlett stepped around the twisted wreck of the door, glaring up at Hanley, all his fears mounting. His hat was off, forgotten on the floor, and the broad streak of white in his hair seemed to have caught the jailer's interest anew. Howlett stopped a pace away. "Something on your mind?"

Hanley continued to watch him, rolling the cud around in his mouth, eyes unwinking. Looking for trouble, Howlett thought, and cocked for it. The girl came up beside Howlett then, and Hanley drew a deep breath.

"Nothin' that won't keep," he said through his teeth. "What're we waitin' on?"

"Grub," Howlett said, moving over to throw a quick look in the wagon. "Nothing's been loaded."

Dollarosa said, "I'll take care of it," and, waiting for Howlett's nod, stepped down.

The girl handed Howlett the shell belt and pistol he had been forced to discard that morning. He clapped the heavy leather around him, anchoring the buckle above his left hip. She gave him his hat. Still keeping Hanley in the reach of his regard, he passed her the six-shooter he'd got from the deputy. "Keep it handy."

"We had better eat first," Frankie said. "You're probably starved."

"It can wait till we come up with the crew. Give Dollarosa a hand, will you, Hanley?"

The jailer slid off his horse without comment. The gambler broke the door loose from its twisted bottom hinge and dragged it out of the way. Howlett unhitched the nickering team and led it off with his buckskin and the other two mounts across the darkening yard. In the barn he forked hay down to them and got each a bucket of oats before leaving.

Hanley, a sack of flour over one shoulder and a sack of potatoes clamped under the same arm, abruptly stopped ten steps from the wagon. Shod hoofs pulsed out of the valley's blue shadows. As Hanley went on and dropped his load in the wagon, Dollarosa came from the house with both arms filled. The sound, plainer now, pulled his head around.

"Company?" Frankie, hurrying, came around the wagon.

"Comin' fast," Hanley said, with a look at Howlett. In silence they watched the horseman take shape and drum into the yard, suddenly veering, hauling up in a slither of dust and flung grit.

"Lippy!" the girl cried.

It was the hand she had sent to the county seat. He was short, a wrinkled wart of a man, looking beat as his horse. "No luck," he grunted, and looked the group over curiously.

"You didn't record it?"

"Never got no further'n the outside of that office." He sleeved an arm over his face, cuffed dust off his pants. "Harry had three of his hound dogs waitin'. Didn't see no point dyin' over somethin' they was goin' to git anyway."

The girl looked at Howlett and went into the house. Yellow light shafted through the windows. "Maybe it's just as well," Hanley breathed. All of them knew he was looking at Howlett. "You can run now, mister, if that's what's been holdin' you."

The gambler, stepping into the breach, said, "Life would be a dull business without Harry Rimrose." Lippy cursed.

"What would he do with Star Cross," Howlett asked, "if he got it? He's already driven half the small owners off their holdings. How much room does he want for his elbows?"

"He wants all of it," Frankie said, coming back.

"An'll probably get it." That was Hanley, still watching Howlett.

Howlett said, "He'll have to walk over a lot of dead bodies."

"Dead bodies," Lippy growled, "is duck soup to that feller. Ain't you heard about this spread?"

"Howlett's another one likes dead bodies." Hanley smiled. "Dead men don't tell."

Howlett turned clear around. "You been throwing the hooks into me ever since we got here. What are you fishing for?"

"Mebbe I don't like the color of your hair. Mebbe I just plain don't like killers."

The man expected trouble and had himself braced for it, one hand wrapped around the handle of his Colt. Howlett moistened his lips, breathing deeply. "You feel like that, why did you come out here?"

Before Whiskers could speak, Dollarosa said: "I'll tell you why. He came because he was told to come. And not just to push cattle."

"Now I'm here," Hanley declared, "I'll do what I please."

"Not quite," Howlett said.

Breath turned scarce. Bird and insect sounds became more noticeable. Dollarosa said, "Jim had an idea it might come in handy to have a little law where you'd be able to get at it."

He was speaking to Howlett but watching

Hanley. "Jim," Hanley sneered, "ain't got all his marbles."

Howlett walked up to him, tight of mouth. "Get it out in the open."

"I don't aim to see you make a fool of that girl." Hanley's look was pale and wild. "I don't know Virgen but I know *your* kind! You didn't want to come here, but once you seen how things shaped up—what a windfall it could be, you started getting in your licks. Played up to the girl, got her to turn the ranch over to you. Baines seen through your game, so you got him off to one side in the dark an'—"

"No!" Frankie's scream tore through his words. "That's not so! Not a single bit of it!"

In the shocked silence no man moved or looked up to meet her eyes, nor could one of them summon the courage to meet the look of either of the others. They stood shamed before such pride and trust; and Howlett, more ashamed, more embarrassed than any, turned and blindly walked into the unseeing shadows.

THIRTEEN

THEY came up with the crew on the long side of ten. They ate, bedded down and were up before dawn, again mauling food, drinking black coffee in the light of the fire. There was very little talk. Virgen laid out the day, saying who would work where, pairing Hanley off with the testy-faced Kidder, putting the gambler with one of the old Tappan hands. After they'd caught up and gone, Virgen, getting into his own saddle, said, "That tinhorn won't earn the damned grub he swallers!"

"Not your worry." Howlett put a hard look on him. "Took you nine months to pick up a couple of hands. I got these two inside of nine minutes. This ain't cow work. Any fool that can sit a horse can push cattle."

Virgen's stare came at him. "You're the boss." He shrugged, and rode after the men. Howlett knew then that he was going to have to watch Virgen even closer than he'd figured. But not, he thought, just yet.

This notion received support when, looking over the gather in the cold gray light of day, he was agreeably surprised to find it larger than expected. Obviously Virgen had driven the men hard, attempting to create a better impression while he waited a break or further orders from Harry Rimrose.

The pair who had stood the last trick as night-hawks rode off in the direction of camp to get their breakfasts and draw fresh mounts. One would be back while the other stayed with Frankie to help move and take care of the re-muda, the saddle pool of spare horses which included everything not presently in use. This was not a regular roundup. There would be no branding, no work for the knife. They were combing the range, sweeping it clean as they went. For this kind of a job, a last-year's bronc would serve as well as another; night horses and cutters would be kept fresh in the pool. The remuda would follow the wagon. When a man's horse was fagged, he'd ride in for another. On impulse Howlett rode after the nighthawks. Virgen could draw whatever conclusions he wanted.

Overtaking the two men, Howlett waved Beauty on, saying to Lippy, "I'm going to have him stay with Miss Frankie." Then he briefly related what had happened in town, the developments brought out at the inquest. "You know anything about Hanley?"

"Never saw him before."

"Knew he was working for Vaguely, didn't you?"

"Heard so."

"Hear anything else I might like to know about?"

"Guess not."

Howlett said bleakly: "You don't know much about me but you certainly know I had nothing to do with persuading Frankie to quitclaim this ranch to me. I'm trying to help her. I need the support of every man on the pay roll."

Lippy said nothing. He rolled up a smoke, licked and lighted it. He stared for a moment, then offered the makings to Howlett, who stared some himself before taking them. Howlett said abruptly, "We haven't got enough boys to hold this range, we haven't got enough even to keep down the rustlers. I don't want her whipsawed out of everything. Only answer I can find is to strip this spread of cattle before Rimrose beats us to it. Bunching them will probably be doing him a favor. We can't help that. Only thing we can do is try and get them to market."

"Where?" Lippy said.

"I heard the lumber crowd up around Flagstaff would buy."

"That's a lot of miles, mister."

"You got a better idea?"

Lippy shook his head.

"I'd be as well pleased if Virgen continues thinking of me as owner."

Lippy nodded. Then Howlett said, "Vaguely claimed at the inquest he lost that trail heading east at a place he called the Barrens. What's beyond?"

"X Bar."

"And beyond X Bar?"

"Two Pole Pumpkin."

The two men stared at each other. "You better watch your step," Lippy grunted. Howlett turned his horse and rode back to the gather.

Virgen was easing the collected herd south. All morning riders continued to come in with fresh bunches of cattle. By dark, with the north third of the range swept bare, they had about twelve hundred head under guard. Driving a mixed herd was going to be hell with the handles off, but they had no choice. Virgen was still giving the orders. Tomorrow, he said, they would clean out the basin.

"I think," Howlett decided, "we'll leave the basin till last. We'll work the south range tomorrow, clean them out of those roughs below the Pass."

Virgen looked around, started to speak, then changed his mind. He stood there a moment stiffly, jerked a curt nod, and struck off for the wagon. The others wearily trailed after him. Dollarosa drifted in beside Howlett. "He didn't like that. You better watch him."

Howlett nodded.

But he was thinking to himself it wasn't Virgen he'd have to watch.

The men bolted their food. Virgen told off Lippy and the fat-bellied Beauty to first trick with the herd, Kidder and himself for second watch, and Howlett and Hanley to wind up the night. The first pair, grumbling, caught up their night ponies and went off to sing them down. A couple of the others rolled smokes. Dollarosa got a cigar going.

Howlett sat with his back against a rock, his restless eyes seeing things in the night that were not visible to others. And he knew it was no good. Resting his arms across his knees, rubbing his rope-burned palms together, he listened to the desultory talk of those around him while he covertly watched the girl finishing up. He saw the faded cotton print, the tired face, and he pressed his lips together tightly as the others sought their blankets. Even Virgen. The foreman made quite a business of it.

Howlett ran a rag through the barrel of his pistol, stared inscrutably across the flames, and replaced the cartridge Frankie had fired. He thought of Star Cross and what it meant to the girl. In his mind he went over the problems that must be solved and the bitter choices he had. It was not yet too late to run.

The fires died down.

Night sounds filtered across a thousand stars, and out on the flats weary voices plaintively mumbled their songs as the fat one and Lippy endlessly circled the bedded herd. Howlett was careful to be quiet going after his blankets, but the girl must have heard him.

"Howlett?"

Just a whisper, but it stopped him, anchoring him as no other thing could have.

"Will!"

He had told her "Will" was what his mother had called him. Hearing it from her shook him with a nameless fear. Sweat came out on him. He turned and saw her by the wagon in a cotton shift, one hand outstretched, her hair tumbled about her shoulders.

She saw the blankets and came toward him. He could see the distraught look of her enormous eyes. "I dreamed that you were leaving . . ." Her fingers gripped his arm.

He stood there, trapped, throat dry as paper.

Her fingers tightened. "Don't—Don't go, Will. . . .I couldn't bear it." She was suddenly crying, her head against his chest. He could feel the warm wetness of her tears, feel her shaking. Helpless and miserable he put an arm around her stiffly. Her face lifted. "You think it matters to me what you've done? That night at Tigley's when you went by in the street on your yellow horse, I knew who you were. It was all in that Texas paper Virgen left in Dad's office. Your picture—the one they took after the Brady sheriff got you away from that mob. That's past; it doesn't master. Look at me. . . . Take hold of me —harder! I won't break, Will. There's nothing in this life I can't face but seeing you go."

Wide awake in his blankets, Howlett lay completely still, watching the ghosts that tramped through the night, watching and waiting, not daring to think, afraid of the future, afraid of himself. Hearing the far mournful wail of the wind, he watched the stars being blotted out mile by mile. Weather was making, but his mind wasn't on it; he was staring aghast at what he had got into, the folly he'd embraced, the pressures that were rushing him blindly, heedlessly headlong into a madness of uncontainable emotions.

All his values and all he had lived by were stripped away. A girl he'd considered plain was suddenly beautiful, bewilderingly precious. And Bill Virgen knew his identity! Moreover, tonight, by countermanding Virgen's orders, he had forced the foreman's hand, creating an issue which in one fashion or another Virgen had to meet swiftly. By changing the location of tomorrow's work he had let the man know . . .

Howlett heard the hoofbeats, knew that Lippy or Beauty was coming in from the herd to wake the second-trick men. He closed his eyes, hearing the horse stop. Boots struck earth and moved tiredly around him, going toward Virgen. The foreman grumbled. Boots went away. Near the grove where stretched ropes held the saddle pool a horse snorted. Hoof thuds passed, fading toward the herd. Kidder's muffled voice sounded, briefly cursing.

Dollarosa's shape lifted onto an elbow as Howlett fully clothed, slipped out of his blankets. "Better rest while you can. They're not like to try anything short of San Carlos—that's where his contracts are."

What he meant, of course, was that Rimrose's beef went to reservation Apaches. Howlett didn't answer. The gambler started to get up. "Stay there," Howlett said. He stood a moment listening. "Which way is Two Pole Pumpkin from here?"

"North. Look." Dollarosa sounded irritable.

"Harry's no fool. We're moving these cows right up where he wants them. He knows Vaguely's watching him. Why should—"

"He'll use Fred Oaks. They can't know where we're bound for. He won't take any chances. Virgen knows I'm onto him. He's got to warn Harry. When Rimrose learns I'm giving the orders, he'll throw Fred Oaks at the herd. He'll guess soon enough when he don't hear from Bill."

Another horse was coming in, the first guard's partner relieved by Virgen and Kidder.

Dollarosa, grunting, came up off the ground. Howlett caught the gambler's arm. "Keep an eye out for Frankie." He was gone before Dollarosa could argue.

It was getting blacker all the time. At the saddle pool Howlett got one of the night horses, a big hammerheaded bay. He struck into an arc that would take him widely around to the north of the bedded cattle. Once he thought he heard the soft fall of hoofs behind him, but when he paused nothing came of it. Imagination, he told himself, knowing the queer pranks taut nerves could play. He tried to relax. Wind bit coldly through his clothes, and he got into his brush jacket, again checking the saddle gun Vaguely had lent him, riding with the weapon out and ready across his pommel. Shooting was the last thing he wanted right now. He would like to have moved farther away from the herd, but he was afraid of losing the man. At least the wind was coming from the cattle to him, but a gun flash bursting out of this murk could send those cows bawling onto their feet. A stampede might help Rimrose; it wouldn't help Frankie.

He thought once more that he heard hoof sounds in back of him, and again he stopped; but with the wind whistling through the grass and mesquite fronds he couldn't be sure of anything.

He went on a bit farther, pulling into the fringe of a thicket of catclaw. The herd was just yonder, unseen but well enough marked by its smell. He dared not approach any nearer; too near would be as bad as too far. It didn't appear reasonable that the man would chance taking off straightaway; but even as he thought, he glimpsed movement to the right of him, a man on a walking horse moving north.

The figures couldn't have been more than thirty feet away when Howlett, levering a shell up for firing, softly called, "Hold it!"

The man stopped so short his horse went back on its haunches.

"Don't try it," Howlett warned. "Let that horse come up now—careful. That's better. Back him over here."

But, instead of complying further, the man yelled, "Bill—Bill!" and, spurring, went for his gun.

FOURTEEN

IT was Kidder.

Howlett, lifting the rifle, shot the horse out from under him.

Kidder fell hard. Thrown clear by the jack-knifing collapse of the extended horse, he went end over end. Howlett had no chance to see what became of him. Out of the confusion, two distinct sounds beat toward him, the nearer stemming from the direction of the herd. Twice powder flashes marked the course of this rider.

He was coming up fast. His second try cut an eerie whine close above Howlett's head. Howlett fired again. The fellow's nag came apart in midstride. With a banshee scream it reared straight up as though bound for the moon, which, briefly appearing through a rent in the clouds, illuminated everything in a garish flood of blue-white light.

Howlett saw Virgen stagger to his feet. The man seemed dazed. He stood half bent over, swaying, staring like a sleep-walking idiot. Both hands, like a scarecrow's, hung slapping and empty. It dawned on Howlett that Virgen was seeking his gun, but the foreman was swept completely out of his thinking as the herd, with dreadful unanimity, came bawling frantically off the ground.

They were pointing west as clouds swirled over the face of the moon. Howlett spurred, desperately lashing the bay with his rein-ends, shaken by the rumble of those thousands of hoofs as he drove the horse through the terrible dark in blind search of a wagon standing square in their path.

Rimrose, quitting town with his crew following the fiasco of their attempt on Howlett after the inquest, was in the clutch of thoughts that were driving him wild. All of his plans were on the brink of disaster. Everything he held dear was falling apart. How could one man inspire such havoc? It didn't make sense, but Howlett was doing it. In Harry's mind was a picture of prison gates—he could almost hear the iron clang of them back of him. Nothing before had ever shaken him so. Already the man had all but taken over Star Cross, had given the girl hope, bolstered the fumbling suspicions of Vaguely, and now was threatening the very core of Two Pole Pumpkin's authority and influence.

The rancher rode in a fine sweat of intolerance. A drifter he'd never even set eyes on before—a meddling nobody! He, Rimrose, had had this camp in the palm of his hand, its shopkeepers quaking with terror, its mine-owners backed to the wall by failure of communications and their own inability either to ship ore in quantity or to get pay rolls past the brigands who appeared to have made Blind Mule their headquarters. Three days ago, had anyone predicted the possibility of his losing his grip, Rimrose would have snorted with contempt. Now there were muttering men on every corner! Three days ago no one would have presumed to question his word on anything. Now they were openly linking his name with all manner of things which had happened to people no longer around—there was even speculation concerning what he'd done with the pay roll taken from Cretch and Crispen!

Why hadn't Virgen killed the son of a bitch!

Had he let Bill get too high on the hog? By God, there would be a hereafter for some of these fools! A mighty sorry awakening—but that could wait. A first-class example was the thing needed now, and Star Cross would furnish it. When he was done with Howlett and Frances Tappen, Vaguely and the rest of these bastardly ingrates would be hunting their holes in one hell of a hurry!

No quarter—that was the ticket. He would pick up Oaks and some other key men. . .

Back in town, Jim Vaguely was a jittery man. That inquest had really stirred things up, and the attempt to cut Howlett down in the street had made a considerable change in people's thinking. Rimrose's name was being bruited around openly. A pair of local hardcases had been snatched up by a citizens' committee of miners, flogged, tarred and feathered and ridden out of the camp on rails. Rimrose was bound to retaliate. Armed miners in groups were patrolling the town. Five ruffians without visible means of support had been dragged out of saloons in the last half-hour, flogged and told to get out of the country. A delegation of miners stood in front of the jail making sure Jim Vaguely stayed right where he was. Orso sat nursing his double-barreled Greener. O'Mansky grinned cheerfully. "Don't look so glum. It's a good job they're doin', and what I say is, more power to 'em."

Vaguely shook his head. "Harry won't take this layin' down. He's going to see that feller Howlett back of everything that's happenin'. It's goin' to fetch him down on the girl."

"Still," O'Mansky said after thinking about it, "what can he do?"

"He can rub them out and Star Cross with them."

"Oh, come now," the gunsmith protested. "Considerin' the temper of this camp, he certainly wouldn't dare pull anything as raw as that." He slapped the deputy's leg. "What you need's a drink."

"By grab, I'm serious," Vaguely growled. "From where Harry sits this camp's in need of a frightening example. Put yourself in his place. He's got all the toughs in this country back of him; inside of two hours he can be ridin' with thirty men at his back. And when he gets through with Star Cross he'll come here."

O'Mansky quit grinning. "Give me one of

them Winchesters," he said, getting up.

The deputy looked grim. "Three men ain't goin' to amount to much. What this needs is a first-class posse."

"Most of them boys out front is sober," O'Mansky decided, peering through the window. "I don't know how many of 'em's ever been in a saddle but . . ."

Bill Virgen could hardly credit his luck when Howlett, reins flying, went crashing off through the dark. He had counted himself a dead man when he'd come up from that spill with both hands empty, and the fact that he wasn't took a bit of getting used to. He pulled great breaths of air into his lungs, flexing the slabs of his shoulders. "Goddam peckerneck!" He spat, scowling around him, and bent over and picked up the six-shooter he hadn't dared make a pass for with Howlett's eyes blazing down at him. He whacked the barrel against his leg to knock out any dirt it might have had stubbed into it. He could guess what had sent Howlett larruping off, but he found it hard to comprehend how any guy with all his buttons could be such a screaming ninny. What if the goddam cows did run over her? The world was full of women.

With Bill it would always be first things first, and the first thing Howlett should have worried about was Virgen—as he'd damn' well find out before, by God, Bill got through with him!

He was about to look for Kidder when the moon, again shafting down through the blackness, disclosed the man plodding toward him. The gunfighter was just rounding some brambly mesquite, afoot and without his rifle. There was blood on his face, and his clothes looked as though he'd got into barbed wire. Virgen also observed that he was minus his gun harness and, on the heels of this astonishment, discovered the mounted man back of Kidder. It was one of that new pair—the star packer, Hanley, with a grin on his face, and his Winchester focused on Virgen's middle.

"What the hell!" Virgen growled, hoping the fellow hadn't noticed his six-shooter. He tried to edge it behind his leg, not at all liking the way this shaped up.

Hanley's eyes were sharp. "No sense weightin' yourself down with that iron. Just let—" He quit talking right there and, leaning suddenly forward, seemed to be having a fit of some kind. His eyes appeared to be about ready to pop from his head. "That ring—" he cried hoarsely; and Virgen, appallingly reminded of the emerald on his fist and of the dead woman's hand he had hacked the ring from, frantically flung himself aside, at the same time bringing his gun up. Its muzzle stabbed three lurid flashes. The luckless jailer buckled forward, the rifle falling unfired from his grip. He hung like a rag across the withers of his eye-rolling bronc which abruptly stuck its bill in the ground and dumped the man.

Virgen wasn't caught napping. As the horse dropped its head again, the foreman jumped and wrapped both arms about its neck in a bear hug.

The sunfishing horse kicked like a bay steer, squealing and snorting, but Virgen hung onto him till Kidder woke up and came to his assistance.

When they got the horse quieted, Virgen took the reins and stepped abroad. "Hand up that saddle gun," he rapped out at Kidder.

"By Gawd," Kidder said, "you gonna leave me naked?"

"Any guy dumb as you are should be thankful he's alive."

"Jesus Christ!" Kidder said, and looked as ugly as sin, but he handed up the rifle.

Virgen shoved it back in its boot, his pistol still covering the disgruntled leather slapper. "You light out for Rimrose," Virgen told him, "and don't, by God, stop to pick daisies!"

FIFTEEN

LIFE Howlett thought, was like a river of horns. Deceptively placid in its calmer aspects, even tiresomely dull to the point of monotony where it foundered into swamps of brush-choked backwater until some unexpected storm proved it deep with deadly currents as crammed with destruction as this wild stampede.

His mind flashed back across the miles he had traversed, through the horrors and heartache, the lusts and greed and desperate passions which unwantedly had shaped him to this moment of truth. Gone were the cunning deceptions of ego, the blinding desires of self. Now past events stood in their rightful perspective as obstacles fashioned by a watchful Almighty—challenges to test what mettle a man had in him. They were not unique with Howlett, as he had believed in his rebellion, but rather, in one manner or another, stumbling blocks each in his own time and experience must encounter.

The frustrations he had known were but facets of the universal pattern, a more subtle set of trials by which the Master Alchemist would fetch true ore from dross. Even such talent as

Howlett had shown, and so often and bitterly cursed, was his to use for good or bad, his to account for in the final reckoning. It was not what a man had, but what he did with it. He hoped the scales hadn't tipped too far.

The landscape reeled and tottered under the skittering play of distant lightning. No rain came down, but thunder crashed, prolonged reverberations hollowly smashing across the rip of wind like hell emigrating on cartwheels.

Staring over his shoulder, Howlett saw the pounding mass of frightened flesh and clacking horns which his mad pace—coming in at a tangent—had put a hundred yards behind. But even as he looked he saw that the cattle were gaining. The bay, running hard, was plainly laboring under the terrible demands of fear and spurs. Its jaws, flecked with saliva, were open, gasping with the tremendous effort it was forced to put forth even to hold its own.

So far the camp had been hidden from Howlett, concealed by the black opacity trapped against earth by the rumbling clouds. Now flames leaped up, outlining the wagon in weird silhouette as an armload of dry stuff was thrown on the coals. Sometimes a thing like that would turn a stampeding herd.

It wasn't turning this one. But those at the camp were aware of their peril, and if they couldn't get away at least the flames would give them some light to shoot by. Shooting was all that was left to them now.

The bay was lagging badly. Twisting around

in the leather, Howlett began to fire into the herd, working the lever until his Winchester had emptied every shell in its magazine. The sea of tossing horns was barely two hundred feet behind the heels of his horse. The fire-gilded spokes of the outfit's wagon still seemed an impossible distance ahead, but Howlett was figuring, with God's help, to make it when the bay flailed a front hoof into a gopher hole. Howlett barely had chance to kick free of the stirrups before momentum flung the horse heels over head.

Howlett, thrown clear, struck hard on his face and shoulder, scrambled frantically up and, pushed by his fears for Frankie, ran a few stumbling steps, gasping, seeing nothing but the whirling heart of the fire yards beyond what desperate strength he could summon. It hadn't occurred to him to think what he could do if he should get there. The urge was the strongest he'd ever known.

He crashed into a rock, struck again with his knees and went down, spilling over it, in a tangle of arms and legs. For a moment he was stunned, too beat to move, too whipped to care. The throbbing pulse of those wildly drumming hoofs hammered nearer and nearer.

With a kind of sick futility he twisted his head, as though seeing how far short he'd come of reaching his objective might absolve him of further effort. What caught and held his horrified stare was not the camp but a forward-lunging skirted shape limned against the blazing fire.

"Go back!" he yelled, rolling onto his knees,

and swore in frightened anger when she appeared, instead of heeding him, to redouble her efforts. He fumbled for his pistol, but found only an empty holster. He was scrabbling frenziedly around on the ground when he felt the hard gouge of the weapon in his boot and dug out the six-shooter he had taken from Baines.

Muzzle flashes winked from either side of the fire, and Howlett saw steers go down, but the herd kept coming. A big red-and-tan critter directly in front of Howlett, and scarcely fifty feet away, absorbed three of his shots before it dropped. His next caught the animal immediately back of it, piling it up on the flank of the other. He was terribly afraid there wouldn't be time enough. His last shot didn't stop anything, but the boys at the fire must have grasped his intention. Their concentrated fire piled five more on the growing wedge. As he crouched there, trapped with an empty pistol, Frankie, stiff-faced, slid in breathlessly beside him, thrusting a Winchester into his hands. He dropped four cows, missed twice, and got another.

That last shot did it. The bawling herd split, and went by on either side in an earth-shaking thunder of trampling hoofs.

Long after the dust had been carried away, the trembling girl clung, incoherently sobbing, clutching him fiercely, brokenly murmuring his name over and over. Neither of them noticed when the first drops hit; but Howlett, suddenly conscious of the rain, stiffened uneasily, caught in bitter memories of a past that would not let him go.

"Will!" Frankie cried. She must have sensed his withdrawal. Her arms convulsively tightened. Her head tipped back. Staring into the pale wetness of that upturned face, Howlett groaned deep within him. How—feeling the fright that had turned her rigid—could he do this? Yet he knew that he must—it was like a knife twisting in him. His heart cried out, but he had nothing to offer any woman but constant misery—long nights of terror when he'd be out somewhere away from her and she'd be waiting, never knowing, and at the end of all that torture the final blow—death, and the memory of a bullet-torn body.

He should have gone at once, as soon as she'd got him out of that jail. Instead he'd let her bring him here, and now he couldn't leave, couldn't run out on her even if they'd let him—chained by the love he could never declare, held by the trust he was bound to destroy.

He could hear booted feet slogging toward them from the fire. The sharp, brutal way would be best. He prayed for the courage, then jerked her arms from his neck and shoved her roughly back, away from him.

He forced a sneer into his voice. "Better hunt you up another sucker—that ain't buying you nothing with me. I've slept with the best, and there ain't no woman made that's worth getting the goddam life shot out of you!"

He saw the girl recoil; his eyes filled with a

pity she couldn't see any more than he could see her face in this dark; but he could sense her shock in the way one hand crept up to stop at her throat. She was too proud to cry out. He'd got that much right.

The boots came up, and Dollarosa said: "Hell of a thing—begging your pardon, ma'am. Beauty's gone. The wagon's wrecked. Lippy's back there hunting for that pair of new sleeve garters he picked up at the county . . ." He glanced at Howlett sharply, looked at the girl, but kept his thoughts to himself. "We won't get much good out of standing around here." He bent round to wring out the tails of his coat. The rain came down steadily. He took off his silk tile and peered at it, sighing. "I'm afraid this hat will never be the same again."

Howlett said thinly, "We better get moving."

The rain had put out the fire. Lippy, when they reached what was left of the camp, said disgustedly, "Ain't a damn' horse within ten miles."

Howlett shrugged. "What about Beauty?"

"He went after them cows. He still had hold of his bronc when that hullabaloo started." He peered curiously at Howlett. "You see what set'em off?"

"Virgen was figuring to send Kidder after Rimrose. I put them both afoot."

Lippy glanced around uneasily. "Mebbe we better—"

Dollarosa cut him off with a suddenly lifted hand. "Could of sworn I heard a horse. . . ."

They stood cold and shivering, listening into the steady drip of the rain. "Must have imagined it," the gambler said finally, shaking his head.

Howlett, thinking of Frankie, questioned Lippy: "How far to the nearest shelter?"

"There's that old shack used to belong to Belle Bugle over on Half Mile Creek. . . . Take us most of two hours in this kinda—" He looked at the girl. "Mebbe we better forget that place."

"Why?" Howlett asked.

When the silence drew out, Lippy said uncomfortably: "Belongs to Rimrose now. Virgen might be there. Mebbe Kidder, too, if they found themselves a ride."

They were staring at one another when Howlett asked suddenly, "Where's that jailer?"

Dollarosa said slowly: "He went out toward the herd. Took off right after you did."

"You sick, ma'am?" Lippy asked.

The girl shook her head.

Howlett said, "I'm going after those rifles," and moved off through the rain.

He had a brushman's unerring sense of direction. He encountered no difficulty locating the cattle he'd knocked down to split the herd. But finding his dropped Winchester and the one the girl had fetched, tramping around through that slop, was something else. The wind had finally died down, but the rain fell with badgering persistence. The country could certainly use it, but the monotonous sound of it was maddening. Or maybe he felt a sense of guilt concerning Frankie; he had a foreboding of disaster. Whatever it

was, he couldn't hide from himself the
knowledge that Rimrose would never let things
rest where that inquest had dropped them. He
was bound to push for a showdown, a powder-
smoke payoff that Howlett knew in his bones
would not be delayed much longer.

He found the rock and the rifles, ran his strip
of rag through the guns and reloaded both mag-
azines with shells he had got from Vaguely. He
reloaded Baines's six-shooter and dropped it
into his holster. He started back toward the
camp, wondering if the gambler had really heard
the sound of a horse back there. He had to make
up his mind on a guess, and this was no time for
guessing. If there was a horseman hidden someplace in the dark, was it Virgen or Hanley or an
advance scout for Rimrose?

That last, at least, he felt he could discard.
When Rimrose arrived they would know about
it. You couldn't tell about Hanley; the fellow
had something in his craw, but Howlett couldn't
see why the man would be wanting to lone-wolf
it out there by himself, cut off from everyone. It
seemed a lot more likely Whiskers had run into
trouble. Howlett's jaws tightened. If Virgen had
a horse, he must have taken it from Hanley. And
nothing else would have kept Virgen here but the
possible chance of paying off some black grudge.

More afraid than ever, Howlett struck out for
camp.

A rifle went off, smearing its streak through
the rain. Howlett stopped in his tracks, hearing a
hubbub of voices break out up ahead—Lippy's

frightened cursing, Dollarosa's sharp challenge. Muzzle flashes winked again through the murk. Howlett heard the slug, and knew the camp wasn't the target. He emptied one of the Winchesters and began running, slipping and reeling through the treacherous mud.

There were no more shots. Dollarosa called out, and Howlett answered, "Virgen—he's not here now."

The others hurried to join him. Howlett gave Frankie the loaded rifle and refilled the other.

"What are you going to do?" Frankie asked.

"I'm going to try to find Hanley."

"Might's well look fer a needle in a haystack," Lippy grumbled.

"If he's down," Howlett said, "he's probably someplace fairly close to where I set that pair afoot. If that fellow was Virgen, Hanley must have run into him."

They hadn't covered forty yards when a voice faltered nervously out of the gloom: "Fer Gawd's sake don't shoot! It's only me—Kidder! I got both paws up—"

"Strike a light," Howlett said.

"I ain't got a dry stitch on me—ain't got no guns, no horse or nothin'." Kidder sounded as though his teeth were chattering. "That goddam Virgen . . ."

Howlett levered a shell into the breech of his rifle. "Stand where you are. Keep gassing. I'm coming up to you."

Kidder seemed really anxious to please. "I

been tryin' to find you—by Gawd, I got enough of that Virgen!"

"Where's Hanley?" Howlett said, feeling him over.

"Virgen gunned him down an' grabbed his horse. Took his saddle gun—"

"Be still!" Dollarosa said. Through the beat of the rain they heard horses approaching. "Star Cross!" someone yelled.

"Beauty!" shouted Lippy. "Over here—over here!"

The fat man rode up with water streaming from his hat. "Great night for ducks." He must have seen the way Frankie's dress was plastered to her. He took off his slicker—the only "fish" in the bunch—and made her get into it. "You better take my horse, too—these other four broncs ain't got no gear on 'em."

Answering Howlett's questions, he said he didn't know what had become of the cattle— "probably scattered to hell an' gone." He'd had his hands full, first off, trying to run down the stampeded remuda. He'd been jumped by a big bunch of riders: "Couple dozen of 'em, I reckon. Rimrose was with 'em. They never got close enough to know I hadn't nothin' with me but a jag of loose ponies. Reckon they figured they was treein' Star Cross. I lost 'em off in the roughs, shoutin' an' swearin'—them boys was really cuttin' loose! One of them slugs come so close it raised a blister."

They'd be back, Howlett knew. "We'd better

find that shack," he said. They set off, Dollarosa riding double with Kidder, all of them keeping their eyes out for Rimrose. The man couldn't quit; he was into this thing too deep now. The man was bound to hunt them down, and Virgen would be out there somewhere, keeping track of them. The best they could look for was some place where they could sell their lives dearly.

SIXTEEN

THE rain had stopped by the time they reached the shack.

It was a dismal monument to failure. The corral looked like a drunkard's dream: most of the posts were either wobbly or canted, half the rails down at one end or both, and all of them riddled by wood-boring beetles. The shack—it had once been a two-room log cabin—was reduced by neglect or abuse to four walls, the caved-in roof cluttering most of the floor. But it was shelter, and better, Howlett thought, than nothing. At least the logs were still solid, and too soaked to catch fire.

"We'll have to turn these broncs loose," the gambler said, matter of factly.

Howlett nodded. Kidder opened his mouth as though to protest, but apparently thought better of it. He rubbed his hands nervously across the wet legs of his pants. "Don't I rate a gun?"

Howlett's look passed around. "Anybody got an extra?"

Distrust was apparent in the way they all stood there. Frankie said finally, "You can have this," and held out the six-shooter Vaguely had lent to Howlett. Kidder limped over and took the gun, his look ugly.

"Any man," Howlett said, "is entitled to one mistake." Turning away, he spoke to the gambler.

Howlett put Kidder and Lippy and the fat man to cleaning the debris off the floor of the shack. "Pile the broken timbers outside, underneath the windows, and dump the rest of that stuff on top of them. If it comes to a rush, that'll slow 'em down some, and maybe give us a chance to pick off a few more." The gambler had got rid of the horses. "Dollarosa, you come with me." Stars were coming through the gray twist of the clouds as the gambler followed him over to the corral. "No door on that place," Howlett said. "We'll scatter some of these posts and poles out in front of it." Ten minutes later, working at top speed, they had a pretty fair entanglement spread about the front of the cabin. "Rest of those posts we'll stack up inside. Moon'll be out; they'll probably see this, but they can't watch their feet and do much shooting."

They lugged in what were left of the posts and stacked them up against the doorframe, blocking the opening to a height of four feet. "Keep a little of that lead from plowing through here," the gambler said, brushing his clothes off. They were all uncomfortably damp even now, but the work had taken some of the chill from their bodies. There were three window holes in the cabin; one in the wall of the door facing south, one about eight feet to the right of this in the west wall of the main room, and one in the back room facing north.

Howlett stationed Beauty back there with Frankie to keep the guns loaded for him, checking to make sure they had plenty of cartridges. Kidder he put on the west window with Lippy. "Let's use a little horse sense about this. It could be damn' rough if they bust in here and catch us with our shooting irons empty."

The most vulnerable point, the barricaded door, he kept for himself, giving Dollarosa the front window. Beauty, the gambler, Lippy and Howlett all had Winchesters in addition to their belt guns. They had between them perhaps two hundred rounds of ammunition. As Howlett pointed out rather grimly, "There's none to waste."

There was nothing for any of them to do now but wait.

He didn't honestly see how they were going to get out of this. If, as Beauty had indicated, Rimrose had about two dozen men with him, sooner or later they were bound to get in here. He reckoned he should have sent someone for help, even though he had figured it couldn't do any good. Time was against them. Vaguely, had he known of their predicament, would have probably sent help, but by the time any help could get back here from town the fight would be over. They couldn't hold out for long on two hundred rounds with five of them firing and a full gun for Frankie—not with the kind of odds they were up against. Frankie would have been the logical one to send, but after that business in the kitchen with Virgen he'd been afraid. . . . There was no help for it now; they'd got rid of the horses.

The moon broke through, dappling the range with blue and silver, picking out distant objects with surprising clarity in the washed air, but Howlett knew how deceptive the moon could be to shoot by. He glanced around at the others, finding them settled in their places, and wished Rimrose would get a wiggle on. Thinking and waiting could make a man frantic.

Rifle in hand, Howlett lounged by the doorframe, his sharp and restless eyes searching the blue shadows for movement. He wondered if, when they arrived, he should call out to Rimrose, offering to face him, man to man, just the two of them; but he shook his head, plainly seeing its futility. The man would probably jump at the chance to get Howlett out there where his crowd could drive slugs at him. There was no possibility of such a move helping the rest of them. Rimrose had to kill them all.

Face to face with the inevitable, Howlett deeply regretted the lying words he'd told Frankie; they were as useless as everything else he had done. The need to seek her out, baring his true feelings, frankly admitting her place in his affections, was suddenly so overpowering he half turned away and was starting toward her when Kidder, a black smudge beside the room's bright west window, came upright, firing into the night.

"Christ—they mighta gone by!" Lippy snarled, slamming into him. But the damage was done.

All hell broke loose.

Jim Vaguely was sharper than he appeared. The greater part of his adult life had been spent in one kind of law job or another, and if there was one thing which those years had rubbed off on him, along with the caution which had grown to be a kind of religion, it was an ability to see a little deeper than most behind the various false fronts with which his contemporaries sought to bamboozle themselves and one another. The miners had been stirred up, but most of their talk only went skin deep and, taken by and large, they were not the kind of material he would have picked for the job in hand. But he went out into the street with O'Mansky and called for volunteers. Twenty men surged forward, loud talking, obstreperous. Vaguely held up a hand.

"Just a minute," he said. "It ain't for patrollin' this town I want a posse. Star Cross is in trouble. I've got to go out there and stop Harry Rimrose—"

He lost half of them right there. Grousing about Rimrose and facing the man over the barrel of a gun were two different things. He wound up with six men, and lost two more to indignant wives. O'Mansky swore in disgust.

They combed the saloons, and after talking themselves hoarse swore five more men in. They called on the merchants and clerks and got another three. Five hours slid by before, indifferently mounted, Vaguely led his posse of thirteen deputies out of town. At the forks of the road Ollie Herman suddenly remembered a promise he had made to his girl. That left twleve. Plowing through shale, coming down to Vetner's Creek, Eli Bretterman's sorrel went lame, and then there were eleven.

When the rain began to fall, shortly before midnight, they were still six miles from Star Cross headquarters.

In that first awful moment it seemed to Howlett the night was filled with shooting, spurring, shouting riders hurtling past with all the racket of Indians. Around the cabin they raced in waves. Slugs came through the window openings and door with the sound of angry hornets, chunking into the log walls, one occasionally screaming in wild ricochet. Star Cross hugged the floor, reaching up for the most part to fire without looking.

Howlett opened his mouth to yell at them, but telling them to quit wasting lead wouldn't stop them. They'd level off, give them time. Firing at a man wasn't like shooting rabbits. It was something you had to get used to.

The firing slacked off outside, and he took a look. Back out of range, Rimrose's bunch was dismounting. He could see them scattering through the brush, taking up the positions from which they'd creep in again. They had all the time in the world to get this job done. Back of

Howlett, Lippy said, "I wisht to hell I had a drink!" They would all be wanting one before long. Gunfire did that to you. It did a lot of things to you the books never mentioned.

He made out Rimrose's voice. Very cool—casual almost—it came out of the blue shadows. "Howlett! You hear me?"

"Speak your piece," Howlett said.

"No point in a lot of needless slaughter. My fight's with you. Step out and we'll settle it."

"No!" Frankie cried from the back room.

"Send her out with her arms up and she can leave right now. And any of the others that want to."

"Yeah," Lippy yelled, "in a pig's eye we can!"

Someone outside snickered. The sound was closer than Howlett had anticipated, and he understood then what was behind Rimrose's talk. "Watch out," Howlett growled, "that bunch is creeping in."

Guns began cracking. Little yellow and purple lances of muzzle flame began to spit lead outside every window. Virgen shouted, and horses drummed across the yard. This time they came in a wild rush for the door.

Howlett dropped backward, sinking behind the piled posts, and laid his quick fire at them. Bullets slammed all around him. One drove into the stacked posts of the barricade, knocking the top one off the pile so that it struck his crouched shape, very nearly upsetting him. Across the room Lippy's voice tore upward sharply. Outside, three riderless horses fled, and the attack veered off, with Virgen wickedly cursing. Now the dismounted men, close up with rifles, were making the windows too dangerous to fire from. Howlett saw a shape streaking toward the blank east wall. He drove two shots at the blur and saw the man break and go down.

Two men ran past the door. He got one of them. The gambler's gun was cracking spitefully over Howlett's shoulder. The second man stumbled and pitched, twisting, yelling wildly. Suddenly Frankie was at Howlett's side, holding a Winchester, and the yard out front was filled with floundering, cursing shapes trying to get through the rails and posts.

Dollarosa grunted like a man hard hit. Somewhere Beauty was shouting "God damn!" over and over, and Howlett let go of his empty rifle, reaching hipward as Frankie, screaming into his ear, shoved him frantically.

Whirling, off balance, Howlett heard a bullet whack viciously into a post. Twisting, he saw Kidder's bared teeth—the glint of metal as the man threw down for another try.

Howlett fired from the hip.

Kidder lurched, left arm pawing out as he staggered into the wall. He tried to bring up his gun, was driven forward uncontrollably as lead, coming through the west window, smashed him to his knees. He swayed there, gagging, and abruptly collapsed.

Dollarosa was down. "They're all out front!" Beauty snarled, coming out of the smoke and snatching up Kidder's pistol. Frankie was tight-faced, working the rifle when Rimrose, stepping out of the unguarded back room, suddenly appeared behind Beauty. While Howlett stood locked in paralysis, Virgen's head and great slabs of shoulders came through the west window with a leveled gun.

The gold tooth gleamed in a triumphant grimace. Something in Howlett's frozen look spun Beauty completely around; the captured pistol, whacking into the wall, was torn from his grip. Rimrose, now exposed, had been trying to get a clear shot at Howlett, but the fat man's move had put the puncher squarely in front of that lifting muzzle. If, to save himself, Howlett tried for Virgen, Beauty would die under Rimrose's gun.

Howlett fired at the rancher, and saw Harry's jaw spring wide. Something crashed into Howlett, whirling him about. One spur, driven into a crack between boards, brought him down. He rolled, coming up on an elbow as Virgen's second slug splintered into the floor. Howlett fired again. That shot, angling upward, took Virgen in the groin, jolting him backward. Howlett fired once more, and Virgen dropped in a heap.

As if from a long way off, Howlett was conscious of shouting and a racket of hoofs. The shack seemed abruptly to be filled with dark shapes. He thought they were phantoms until he heard Vaguely's voice. "By grab," the deputy was saying, "you have sure saved the county—"

But Howlett didn't hear the rest of it. Moonlight, as someone worked to get his shirt off, revealed a face very close to his own. "Will—Will . . ."

"You still care?"

"Of course she cares!" Vaguely snapped. "You may be red-striped hell when it comes to a pistol, but you sure got a lot to learn about women. Now lay back there so I can git this took care of!"